What the critics are saying...

Mary Wine's Tortoise Tango is laugh out loud fun! From their first meeting, Joe and Amber shoot sparks off one another. The author has a wonderful sense of humor that comes out with each new adventure. Do not miss this book! A recommended red from ~ *Fallen Angel Reviews*

D1484486

MARY WINE

TORTOISE TANGO

ELLORA'S CAVE
ROMANTICA PUBLISHING

An Ellora's Cave Romantica Publication

www.ellorascave.com

Tortoise Tango

ISBN # 1419953052
ALL RIGHTS RESERVED.
Tortoise Tango Copyright© 2005 Mary Wine
Edited by: Sue-Ellen Gower
Cover art by: Lissa

Electronic book Publication: June, 2005
Trade paperback Publication: December, 2005

Excerpt from *Beyond Boundaries* Copyright © Mary Wine, 2005

Warning:

The following material contains graphic sexual content meant for mature readers. *Tortoise Tango* has been rated *E-rotic* by a minimum of three independent reviewers.

Ellora's Cave Publishing offers three levels of Romantica™ reading entertainment: S (S-ensuous), E (E-rotic), and X (X-treme).

S-*ensuous* love scenes are explicit and leave nothing to the imagination.

E-*rotic* love scenes are explicit, leave nothing to the imagination, and are high in volume per the overall word count. In addition, some E-rated titles might contain fantasy material that some readers find objectionable, such as bondage, submission, same sex encounters, forced seductions, etc. E-rated titles are the most graphic titles we carry; it is common, for instance, for an author to use words such as "fucking", "cock", "pussy", etc., within their work of literature.

X-*treme* titles differ from E-rated titles only in plot premise and storyline execution. Unlike E-rated titles, stories designated with the letter X tend to contain controversial subject matter not for the faint of heart.

Also by Mary Wine:

A Wish, A Kiss, A Dream anthology

Alcandian Quest

Beyond Boundaries

Dream Shadow

Dream Specter

Dream Surrender

Ellora's Cavemen: Tales from the Temple III (Anthology)

Tortoise Tango

Trademarks Acknowledgement

The author acknowledges the trademarked status and trademark owners of the following wordmarks mentioned in this work of fiction:

Hummer: AM General Corporation

Home Depot: Homer TLC, Inc.

Honda: Honda Giken Kogyo Kabushiki Kaisha (Honda Motor Co., Ltd.)

Chapter One

"Hurricane Ruth has reached gale-force winds and is currently bearing down on the Texas coastline. All residents of Pullman County are strongly urged to evacuate immediately."

"No kidding." Amber tightened her hands on the steering wheel as the wind pushed her car about like a toy. Great. Neat. Wonderful. Another gust caught the mini-SUV and she frantically turned the wheel to avoid spinning across the highway like a toy top.

A groan of pure frustration escaped her lips as she righted the car. Punching her foot down onto the accelerator, Amber aimed her vehicle away from the approaching storm.

Some five hours later, Amber lifted weary eyes towards a roadside diner's neon sign. Coffee. Even the word tasted good at the moment.

"You evacuating, honey?" A plump waitress offered a kindly smile with her question. Amber reached a hand up to smooth over her hair before she aimed a grin back at the woman.

"Do I look that bad?"

"Well, pitiful suits you a bit more to my way of thinking. Ladies' room is in the back."

Tossing a muttered "thank-you" over her shoulder, Amber fumbled around in her purse for a hairbrush. Well, she was yet again an honest-to-goodness refugee.

The first true hurricane to hit southern Texas in forty-one years and she, Amber Talisman, managed to move into town just one week before it hit!

Great. Neat. Wonderful.

She was from California! Southern California girls just weren't taught how to secure a house for a hurricane! Or how to drive in one. Well, away from one anyway, in this case. Now, duck and cover during an earthquake, no problem. Hurricane with gale-force winds, big problem!

All right, girl, get a grip. You're still in one piece. Amber glared at her reflection and snorted. She always made it through. Being alive didn't count. There must be a law against curses that forced the victim to live through every single natural disaster known to man.

Dropping her hairbrush, Amber headed back out into the diner and towards coffee. Getting frustrated wouldn't matter. So, she would go placate her lousy attitude with coffee. Hot, steaming java. Today she'd splurge and use cream. Escaping a hurricane definitely earned her some real, cholesterol-laden cream.

Her thighs could go straight to hell.

* * * * *

People were idiots.

Contained in those three little words was the complete and total key to understanding humanity. The true reason that the adult human male produced millions of sperm was to ensure that the species didn't die out from its own ignorance.

"Joe? You see it yet?"

How in the hell could he miss it? This wasn't a traffic accident, it was a quarter-mile of tangled wreckage. More than one of these fools would be getting their auto insurance canceled after this one! Lifting his shoulder, Joe spoke into the microphone sitting there.

"Ten-four. I'm on scene. Better call over to Edwards County General and let them know they've got incoming."

"A right-o on that, Joe." Joe closed his eyes and shook his head. Professionalism. A rather simple concept that not a single civilian member of his staff seem able to apply in the performance of their duties. Straightening his frame out of his patrol unit, he ran a critical eye over his traffic accident.

Twenty-plus passenger cars, two big rigs, the twisted remains of a couple of motorcycles, a boat and a horse trailer.

In fact, there was an amazing amount of cussing filling the air. Instead of screaming for help, his residents were currently trying to decide just who was the bigger jackass. Maybe it was a darn good thing that so many of the cars were wrecked completely. That meant most of the locals' shotguns were pinned in the tangled mess.

"Calvin, you're a toad-faced idiot! Who taught you to drive? Your sister?"

"No! But yours taught *me* how to ride!"

"You bastard!"

"Don't you dare insult my mother!"

And that was Pullman County, Texas, for you. The only highway into town was littered with wreckage and the survivors were too busy brawling to recognize they were the luckiest damn souls on the planet.

An hour later, the only people left were rejoicing about the record pileup. Every tow truck driver within a hundred miles had beaten a path to the accident site and was currently loading as many demolished cars as possible onto their trucks.

Very few of the owners were left. Most ended up at the local hospital. Just whether or not their injuries came from the accident or the following...discussion would have to be sorted out later. Right now, Joe wanted his highway reopened.

Raking his hand across his face he indulged in a single moment of rest. Sleep was very tempting. Forcing his eyelids open, he glared at the few vehicles still littering the shoulder of the highway. The sooner he got them cleared, the sooner he'd get some rest.

Amber glared at a tow truck driver. The man wiped his nose on his sleeve and turned away from her look. Shrugging her shoulders, she turned her attention to another driver. This one was haggling with a potbellied man over the price of towing his smashed Honda away. Another driver appeared and issued a lower bid that the potbellied man instantly accepted. Amber batted her eyelashes but the outbid driver turned towards another bid war and immediately joined it.

"Excuse me. Is there a reason you're still standing here?"

Amber shrieked and turned around to face her company. She tipped her head back and glared at the man. "Do you have to sneak up on me like that?"

"Maybe you should pay attention to what's going on around you."

"Excuse me." She batted her eyelashes and pushed her lips into a pout. Joe cocked his head to study her. He didn't need a smart mouth. Especially not right now. One huge hurricane and a thousand idiotic residents meant he didn't have a scrap of patience left.

"You need to leave, now."

"I would love to. But I'm waiting for a tow truck just like everyone else."

"You were involved in this accident?"

"Do I look like I'm here to sell popcorn?" His eyes narrowed and Amber almost laughed. She clamped her lips closed and tried to keep her face straight. Oh Lord, she really had hit her head harder than that paramedic thought she did!

Because only a complete nutcase would bait the sheriff who was going to be writing up the accident report.

But it was still funny. The sheriff didn't think so. His lips thinned as Amber swallowed another giggle.

"Where is your car?" Joe forced each word out in a flat voice. The woman was laughing at him. He could see it in her eyes. The sky-blue orbs were sparkling just like a Christmas tree.

"I'm on the lower level." She lifted a slim hand and pointed over the embankment. The highway was some thirty feet above the desert floor. The side of the road gave way to a steep dirt embankment. The back of a green SUV was sticking up from its landing spot among the sand.

"Well, that took some doing." The words were out of his mouth before his common sense could stop him. The little lady in front of him didn't find his comment very flattering. Her face flushed with anger before she propped her hands onto her hips. The posture thrust her breasts forward, making the plump curves the center of attention. Well, maybe just the center of his attention but Joe took a single moment to look over those mounds before forcing his eyes back to the explosion of temper covering her face.

"There's not a mark on my car because at least I was watching the road! But these drivers say I'm not a priority and my car has to wait. So maybe you should tell one of them to get over here and I'll be happy to get out of your way."

"Don't need to ask if that's your real red hair." Or her real breasts. A man could spot the fake ones. This pair bounced and moved just right...the way nature designed them to. Joe made a sweep over her left hand before giving in to the urge to look back at her tits. No ring and that gave him far too many ideas about her ample chest.

"OHHHH! It's auburn! My hair is auburn, not red!" Her hands curled into fists because...because that sheriff was grinning like a...a...man! Ohhhh! It wasn't her fault that Texans couldn't drive. "Why doesn't anyone want to haul my car up to this road anyway? I have a credit card."

"But you don't have any damage."

Amber shook her head and glared at the grin that was still sitting on his firm mouth. "What does that have to do with it?"

"All these guys get a cut from the shop they haul their loads to. No damage means no cut."

Amber looked around to see that only a single tow truck remained. The driver was dragging the one remaining car onto his bed. The man tugged his baseball cap down over his head to avoid looking at her. "Are they just going to leave me here?"

Joe crossed his arms and pressed his lips together. Now, coming from most women that phrase might have sounded pitiful. Instead this little redhead looked like she was considering instigating a second brawl if she didn't get the right answer to her question. The last driver hooked a final chain into his prize and raised his head up before catching her look. The man all but raced around his truck and jumped into the cab. Her petite frame lunged forward and Joe hooked her arm to hold her back.

The sheriff laughed at her. Amber felt her face flush red as the same color clouded her vision. He was actually laughing at her. The deep rumble was escaping through that smug grin that was still sitting on his rough face. His hand stopped her dead in her tracks. There was a solid strength there that told her his body was as hard-cut as his face. A little curl of heat hit her belly as she considered what he looked like without the uniform.

"Absolutely perfect." Casting a longing look at her car, Amber glared back at the sheriff. "Guess I'm not leaving. So sorry to disappoint you."

"You're leaving because this highway is about to reopen."

"Glad to hear it. I'll be right here waiting for a tow truck."

"Well, that won't be until tomorrow so I'll give you a ride into town." Joe didn't mind a bit. In fact, he was looking forward to a little more time with his spunky redhead.

"Tomorrow?" Amber caught her lower lip between her teeth and considered her car again. "I can't wait until tomorrow."

"It'll have to. We've got some County trucks but they're all beat tired after sweet Ruth did her worst on this area. Your car isn't blocking traffic so it's not a priority."

"I can't leave my pet here until tomorrow."

Joe watched as the woman cast a worried look down at her car. Well, who said it was just guys that got attached to their wheels? This little lady looked like a mother that was sending her toddler off to preschool for the very first time.

And she was a little lady. Her body was small and compact. But her worn jeans stretched over some very curvy hips. Joe ran his eyes over them again. A woman needed curves if you asked him. Especially right there on her bottom. Little Red had a real nice seat to go with those tits.

"Let's go, Ms…?"

"Talisman and I'm not leaving Flamingo."

"It's a machine not a person."

The sheriff hooked his hand around her arm again and Amber dug her feet into the soft, water-soaked ground. He dragged her forward anyway. In fact, it was almost effortless. The man seemed to possess plenty of strength for the task.

"My pet is down there!"

"You left an animal in a closed car?" Joe felt his temper return in full force. "It could be close to ninety degrees in that car right now!"

"Flamingo likes it hot. But I can't leave him overnight. He's very sensitive to the cold."

"There are laws against leaving an animal in a closed car! Why in the hell didn't you say something? Your mouth seems to work just fine."

Mr. Grouchy Sheriff wasn't just grouchy any longer. The man was stone-cold furious. It wasn't something Amber enjoyed having aimed at her. The anger practically zipped through the air. She pulled a deep breath into her lungs and shoved her own temper aside. The man thought she'd mistreated an animal. That was a good trait in any human, even a grouchy, obnoxious sheriff.

"Flamingo is a reptile and they need the temperature above seventy-five degrees. That is why I left Flamingo in the car. It's too chilly out here for a reptile."

"What kind of reptile?"

"Flamingo is a tortoise. They need it warm, any veterinarian can tell you that."

The sheriff cast a long look at her car before he ran the same considering look over her. His eyes touched every curve before rising to hers again. Amber felt her mouth go dry—this man noticed details. She shivered as she thought about the kind of details he was noticing on those long looks down her body. "You can bet I'll be asking about that fact. For now, go and get her so I can get this road open."

"Flamingo's too big for me to haul up here. I need a tow truck."

"Look, lady, There happens to be three thousand residents stuck behind this accident and I assure you they aren't in the mood to listen to excuses. Get that animal up here now!"

"I'm not strong enough." And Amber really hated having to admit that out loud! The sheriff considered her from beneath his brows for a moment.

"Fine. I'll go and get your pet."

"Flamingo's too big for you to carry up a hill, too."

Oh, now she'd gone too far. Amber watched the man's face cloud with indignant male pride. He actually growled. The sound was low and deep. Half a second later he was headed down the slope towards her car. If Amber had any concept of body language, his said she was in deep trouble now.

Well, that wouldn't last very long.

Too heavy? Like hell. It was just a turtle! His highway was being kept closed by a turtle. And Little Red didn't think he could haul a *turtle* up the hillside. The day he couldn't haul a lousy turtle forty paces was the day he would sign his own death certificate.

Digging his boots into the water-soaked sand, Joe reached for the rear door of the SUV. Yanking it open he peered into the cargo space and shook his head in disbelief. Flamingo was the biggest damn turtle he'd ever seen. The thing took up half of the cargo space the mini-SUV offered. Dull brown with a shell that was at least three feet across and two feet wide. The animal's head was as big as his fist.

Why did everything in Texas have to be bigger?

Chapter Two

Amber waited for the motel room door to close. Her ears registered the small click it made as the lock snapped into place.

Then she let loose.

Rolling onto her back, the room's mattress bounced as her body hit it. Her entire body shook as she finally let out her laughter.

Oooh, but the look on that grouchy man's face had been priceless! Amber kicked her legs into the air as she continued laughing. Big stud that he was, he'd carried Flamingo up that hillside, just to prove how incredibly manly he was.

Wiping a tear from her eye, Amber rolled over and looked at her pet. Flamingo was currently eyeing the motel room with a complete lack of enthusiasm.

"Mama really loves you." The tortoise blinked his reptilian eyes before beginning to walk about searching for a good spot to spend the night. His shell scraped along the wall, dislodging plaster as it went.

Amber jumped to her feet and hastily rearranged the furniture to protect the walls. Flamingo could easily cut though the soft drywall with his shell. The giant, spurred thigh tortoise was banned from her garage because he was equally destructive to car paint.

All right, maybe Mr. Grouchy was more manly than Amber cared to admit. Flamingo weighed over a hundred pounds and any man who could carry that up a slippery hillside did qualify as manly. It almost bordered on hunk, but a girl really needed to see a man without his shirt before she bestowed the title of hunk on him.

Lord knew the man had the shoulders for it.

Amber allowed her memory exactly ten seconds of recall time before she mentally slapped herself back into real life. Yes, the man was built. He must have at least one award plaque at home for shoulder-lifting or push-ups or whatever else men did to build up their chests.

And his abs were tight. Really tight. *And you, Miss Amber, need to find something else to do with your brain. Slobbering over Mr. Grouchy needed to go! Right now!*

That little curl of heat was back in her belly. The way the man looked at her made her shiver. Actually, it was the way he looked her over. Those dark eyes had slid down her body like laser beams and there was absolutely nothing professional about it. It was a primitive form of communication that a blind woman would have understood. Her nipples slowly twisted into little buttons as she felt a moment of feminine pride. Amber shook her head but couldn't stop feeling delighted that a man like the sheriff had been interested in a second look at her.

Heading for the room's shower, Amber decided to indulge in a very long, very hot bath. Always look at the bright side! Yes, her car was stuck in a sand dune. Her house just might be a pile of splinters and the local sheriff was ticked off at her because he'd had to carry her beloved pet up a forty-foot embankment.

Giving the faucet a turn, Amber watched as steam began to rise from the filling tub. Pulling her jeans off, she climbed into the water with a sigh. Okay, being forced to spend the night in a motel room was also another good thing. After all, if her house was still standing, there was bound to be a record amount of yard work waiting for her to do. Instead she was sitting in a hot, steaming bath.

Now that was a bright side, if ever she'd seen one!

Yes, her car was stuck with a capital "S", but it wasn't waiting in line at the local body shop. Her bank account would certainly declare this to be a bright side.

And as for the local sheriff… She hoped he had sore muscles tomorrow morning! It wasn't her fault the man's pride was so thick he'd hauled Flamingo up that hill just to keep from admitting that she was right. Lord forbid any male on the planet agree with a woman. In fact, for all Amber knew that could be a felony in the state of Texas.

Sinking lower into the water, Amber let a naughty little smile creep across her face. Maybe it was too bad she wouldn't get to see Mr. Grouchy again. She needed the comic relief.

Her amusement died quickly as she considered the facts again. Moving to Texas was supposed to dump her into boring, predictable normalcy. So far, life was as crazy as it had been in California. Stepping out of the water, Amber eyed the telephone sitting next to the bed.

Just one little call and she'd be free. At least that was what her mother insisted. But exactly how was Amber to trust that? After all, most people would tell her that she was a crackpot to even believe there was such a thing as curses.

Most people wouldn't believe her if she told them her mother was a witch and proud of it. It wasn't that Amber held any true opinion on her mother's choices, but to cast a curse on her own daughter? What happened to family was family, and I love you despite your Christianity, my dear?

Flamingo snorted as he tried again to dig up the room's carpeting. He raised a harassed look at Amber before tunneling under one of the drapes. Half of his shell disappeared. Running a hand over his shell, Amber gave it a loving pat.

Flamingo had the right idea. It was time for some sleep. Besides, Amber was going to spend at least an hour thanking God for keeping her in one piece today.

And Lord, her mother would just spit if she knew her daughter was praying!

* * * * *

Amber awoke as a fist landed on her door with the force of thunder. She shrieked as she tried to roll out of the bed. The sheets tangled and caught her, leaving her kicking as another couple of knocks landed on the door.

"Just a minute!" Giving the sheet a last kick for good measure, Amber stumbled towards the door. She yanked it open and gasped as the cold morning air hit her.

"Good morning." Another shriek escaped her mouth as Amber slammed the door shut. Oh, why hadn't she checked to see who was at the door?

The door bounced off a firmly planted boot and came swinging in a half second later. Amber raised her eyes to notice Mr. Grouchy was wearing an amused grin this morning. He propped an arm across the doorway and let his grin widen.

"Do you always open the door to just anyone, Ms. Talisman?"

"Maybe I was afraid you were going to put your fist straight through it."

"Maybe." Joe let his eyes slide over what some generous soul might call a top before his eyes touched on a very tempting bare belly. Little Red had a delicious-looking body to go with the curves his mind had already noticed. "Maybe you should secure the chain before turning in for the night."

"Is there a reason you're darkening my doorway?" Tossing her hair over a shoulder, Amber blinked her eyes to clear them. That grin was turning into a smirk as the man's eyes surveyed her. Her skin tightened and Amber pressed her mouth into a firm line. Opening the door while she was half awake was stupid, she just didn't need it pointed out to her.

"The way I see it, you should be rejoicing that it's me. Or were you expecting someone?"

The man glared at her with male smugness. What could she say? His face changed expression momentarily before he extended his hand into the room.

"Jesus! It's hot as hell in there! No wonder you're practically naked!"

This time, Amber managed to get the door slammed shut. She heard the muffled curse that came out of Mr. Grouchy's mouth as the wood hit his hand. She fumbled to turn the lock as her face exploded in color.

Naked? Oh God! She was practically naked. It could get mighty hot in Southern California and her favorite summer pajamas were eight years old and very threadbare now. Chancing a look down, Amber was just grateful the thin cotton was a dark shade of purple or her nipples would be showing through.

"Ms. Talisman, open the door!"

"You can just get lost!"

"If you want your car back, open the door."

The note of firm authority in his voice bothered her almost as much as her own stupidity. But she needed her car back.

The door opened and Joe thrust his hand out to push it completely open. The chain gripped and held as Little Red peeked around from behind it. A small smile lifted her lips as she watched the chain keep the door from opening any further.

"Thanks for the advice."

Joe ground his teeth together. The woman was a menace. Even if it was a misuse of county resources he was going to upgrade her tow call to urgent! Because if he didn't get her out of his county immediately, he was going to strangle her!

"I suggest you get dressed so I can get you back out to your car." Joe didn't wait for a reply. He turned on his heel and headed for his patrol unit.

Amber watched him leave. She slapped a hand over her own cheek as she caught her eyes lingering over the man's shoulders. Boy, he really was the very definition of "hunk".

Kicking the door shut, she frantically grabbed her overnight bag. She really did need that ride out to her car. Better with Mr. Grouchy than some unknown stranger. Yanking a sweater over her head, she ran a brush through her tangled hair.

He was waiting for her. His large frame was propped against the side of his police car. Mr. Grouchy had his arms crossed over his chest and a pair of mirrored sunglasses on. His face was set in pure granite as he watched her door. Stepping out of the room, Amber felt the cool air and sighed in relief.

"If that heater is broken, you should have requested another room for the night."

"It's not broken."

"You want it that hot?" Maybe the woman wasn't a menace, it was possible she was just plain insane.

"I told you that Flamingo is sensitive to the cold."

"You're kidding, right?" Joe pulled his glasses off and walked close enough to see her eyes. "You're telling me, you slept in that hot box so that your turtle would be happy?"

"Flamingo is a tortoise, not a turtle and his heat lamp is in my car."

Joe just couldn't help it. He practically doubled over with laughter. The woman was near naked and panting from heat because she loved her tortoise.

Amber watched the sheriff with growing outrage. Why exactly was it that this man seemed to enjoy laughing at her so much? Sure, she found her own life infinitely amusing but it was her life! Mr. Grouchy was downright rude and her temper quickly bubbled over her limit.

She kicked him.

"He's my pet! Not a thing!"

Joe considered her sweater a moment while his memory recalled her ultrathin pajama top. The sweater was a sack. But his memory was far too good. She had a plump set of tits that made his mouth water.

"Most women get a cat."

"I'm just a mold-breaker."

Slipping his glasses back into place Joe didn't resist the urge to provoke his companion once more. "Well, I've heard that most redheads are different. But naming a male anything Flamingo is low, lady. Very low."

"It's auburn! Did you say we were ready to go?" He sent her a smug grin before pushing away from his post against the police car. Amber shifted back as she noticed just how tall the man was. His heavyset shoulders emphasized the fact. Movement caught her eye and she glanced around to notice that Flamingo was taking his chance to escape the hotel room.

"That thing can move rather fast when it wants to."

Amber narrowed her eyes as he once again called her pet a thing. Flamingo was as affectionate as any dog. Just as much trouble but blissfully silent. Living in the Southern California basin meant your neighbor was most likely only thirty feet away. Lawsuits erupted over excessive barking. Silly or not, her giant tortoise was an ideal pet.

"What are you doing?"

Amber glared at him in response. "I'd think you know an apple when you see one." Dropping the piece of fruit onto the ground, Amber used her booted foot to crush it into several large chucks.

"What I see is a mess. You need a ticket for littering?"

"Well, if you'd rather carry Flamingo over here…fine. But he'll walk himself over if there's an apple involved." Almost on cue her pet caught scent of the fruit and raised his head in Amber's direction. The tortoise moved his body forward on lumbering steps.

It was the damnedest thing he'd ever seen. Joe pulled his glasses off to stare as that turtle immediately beat a path to the broken apple. He stretched out his neck and caught a chunk between his jaws before crushing it. His head stretched out again for one of the remaining pieces. Little Red opened the back door of his car and tossed the two remaining pieces into the footwell of the passenger seat. The creature sniffed the air momentarily before placing two feet into the car as it stretched out its neck for the fruit.

And then Little Red bent over and showed off her perfect bottom for him. Joe felt his mouth go dry as he watched her wrap her arms around her pet's huge shell. Damn, she had one nice ass.

Her boots slipped on the asphalt as she struggled with lifting the animal completely into the car.

"Let me do that!"

Dropping Flamingo with a huff, Amber turned around and bumped into the sheriff. Her body bounced away from him sending her backwards into Flamingo's shell. Her pet gave a loud hiss of displease for being sat on.

The sound must have startled the lawman because he sent Amber spinning away from the car in a split second. Her feet scuffled along the asphalt as she tried to keep her balance.

"Did he bite you?"

"Tortoises don't have teeth." Flipping her hair out of her face, Amber glared at him once more. The man's body was rigid as he eyed her pet. Those eyes shifted back over her and inspected her from top to bottom before he gave a single nod of his head.

"You should have let me pick him up, unless you want your back wrenched out."

"Could we go now?" Because she was really getting tired of dealing with a chauvinist. Flamingo was her pet and she'd take care of him, herself! She certainly didn't need a *man* to help her out.

"By all means!" Joe sent the passenger door closed with a slam behind the snapping sounds of the last piece of apple being eaten. Amber opened the front door and pulled it shut as she tossed her head. Joe couldn't help but laugh. What a stubborn, foolhardy…redhead!

* * * * *

"Well, now, that car is stuck real good." An oil-stained hand reached for the equally stained brim of a baseball cap and tugged on it for the tenth time. "This isn't going to be covered by your auto club."

Amber curled her fingers into a fist before she forced her hand open. When it came to cars, there seemed to be some unspoken law of the universe that made it impossible for men to speak plain English to a woman.

"Would you like a credit card or a check?"

"I normally only take cash."

Of course! Amber considered the stretch of open highway in front of her. The next exit was two miles away and even then, there wasn't any great chance there would be a bank anywhere to be found. They were still a good twenty miles out of town.

Cocking her head back to the opposite direction, she considered the sheriff as he leaned against his car. His eyebrows were dipped over his eyes as he continued to stare at her. Noticing her attention, he raised one arm up form his chest and very deliberately looked at his wristwatch. Crossing his arm back across his chest he resumed his glaring.

Snapping her head around, Amber fixed her sights on the driver. Well, of the two men, she'd take the tow truck driver any day. Her oil-fingered friend would break far faster than the lawman.

"Hmm…I'm so sorry to hear that. The sheriff isn't going to be very happy about his highway being cluttered. But if that's your policy, I'll just have to find someone who can take a credit card." Amber fluttered her eyelids at him "There just isn't a bank anywhere around and a girl just doesn't carry large amounts of cash in her handbag these days. You understand." Flipping around, Amber set her body towards the sheriff. The lawman's frown deepened before he raised his huge frame away from the patrol car. He flexed his hands and moved to meet her as his eyes aimed a harsh look at the driver behind her.

"Well now, I guess I can make an exception and take that check. No need to involve the law." The sheriff was bearing down on him and the driver turned his frame away from the man as he jerked the pull chains free from the bed of his truck. Amber felt a smile tug at her face as she listened to the rattle of the chains.

The soft crunch of gravel hit her ears as Joe stopped directly in front of her. One hand reached for the mirrored glasses and lowered them just an inch so that his eyes could inspect her once again. Amber felt her smile fade as she stood facing his hard face. She forced her head up and refused to shrink in front of him. The tow truck driver's hurried steps were carried right over her head and straight to the sheriff's ears. The lawman shifted his glittering eyes over her shoulder and considered the driver of the tow truck before returning to her face again.

"Your hair is red."

* * * * *

"Good evening, Joshia."

Joe's back came away from its resting place against his office chair in a split second. He watched Terri Clark with a practiced eye as the woman sauntered into his office without knocking. Her lipstick was shining from recent and abundant application. She had a single scrap of paper clutched between her long, fire-engine red fingernails as she wove her way to the surface of his desk.

"This just came in, so I brought it right up."

Joe pulled the pink message slip from her hand before she got close enough to sit on the edge of his desk again. When Terri managed to find an excuse to get into his office, she wouldn't give up the field 'til he left it himself.

"Thank you, Ms. Clark."

Her lips turned into a full pout before she swung around on a high heel and made her way to the door. Her hips swished with abundant motion before she turned her head and sent him a wink.

Joe collapsed back into his chair and raised a hand to his temples. The Pullman County Sheriff's office was a catastrophe. The previous sheriff died in office at the age of eighty-two. The old man hadn't been able to master the civilian personnel that staffed the office.

Terri Clark was just one of several problems. But she was the only one that Joe took personally. Hell, the woman would sit herself smack down on his lap if he didn't stand up when she came through his office door. He'd learned that lesson the hard way, so to speak.

Now if Little Red wanted to sit in his lap, maybe that wouldn't be such a problem. Joe's face turned into a frown. Exactly why was he considering Little Red's company? The woman was hell on wheels.

His office chair squeaked as he sat back down. On impulse, Joe reached for the keyboard and pulled up Little Red's identification. The state-issued driver's license picture popped up along with her basic information. His phone buzzed for attention, so he hit the print option before picking up the receiver.

With his attention diverted to his conversation, Joe turned back to his desk and stared at his printer. The output tray was full of neat, freshly printed papers. An entire stack of them.

Most people had a page or two of official information that was stored with the state or federal government. Traffic violations, maybe a car accident or two. But unless the person had a record, three pages was the max.

Little Red had over ten.

Goddamn it! Grabbing the sheets off the tray, Joe began to discover just where Amber Talisman had begun to go wrong in her life.

Chapter Three

Amber stared at her cell phone for an entire five minutes before picking it up. Her mother's number glared at her from the digital face of the small piece of technology. The phone would ring, then her voice mail would pick up and exactly thirty seconds later, her mother would redial and the phone began ringing again.

Jabbing the send button, Amber set her teeth together as her mother's sunny voice filled her ear.

"Amber Star, just how are you?"

"Hello, Mother. I'm fine, thank you." Amber clamped her teeth together as she listened to her mother's laughter.

"So, when should I expect you home, dear?"

"I am home and, thank God, everything is just fine."

"Amber Star, don't you dare use that word with me!" Her mother wasn't happy any longer. Frustration was clearly expressed through her voice. "Come home and stop being so stubborn!"

"Have a nice day, Mom, and remember, I'm just fine!" Snapping her phone shut, Amber indulged in a moment of self-pity. Actually, all things considered, she was owed an entire hour of self-pity. But she really didn't have time for it right now.

"Do you make a habit of lying to your mother?"

"Jesus!"

Joe considered his newest resident as she rounded on him like a small tornado. That red hair of hers swung out and around her face as she faced off with him.

"Why do you keep sneaking up on me?"

Folding his arms over his chest, Joe cocked his head to look down on her. "When are you going to pay attention to what's going on around you?" Amber glared at him as he stood in her front yard. He'd left the mirrored sunglasses off for a change and she stared at the black eyes that were currently inspecting her. His patrol car was parked just ten feet behind him making it rather stupid of her to have not heard the engine.

"I was a little busy. Sorry."

"Um-hmmm, I guess I can understand that."

The man stopped watching her and began to slowly circle her house. Or, Amber should say, the man was walking around what was left of her house. Her three-room house was now a huge tangled mess of splintered wood and broken glass.

"You have insurance?"

"Of course!"

"Consider yourself lucky. There are a few people discovering that insurance sure would come in handy right now." Joe finished his assessment and turned back towards Little Red. The house was a total loss. If she could salvage the kitchen flatware, she'd be lucky. But Joe found Amber remarkably calm for such a moment. The blue eyes weren't bright with tears and she stood looking over the mess with a rather calm acceptance reflected on her face.

"Well, I don't think my insurance company is going to feel so lucky when they get the news that my house is a pile of splinters."

"I'm surprised you have an insurance company."

Oh…Amber knew that tone. There was no mistaking it. The lawman had been checking up on her. "Insurance is required when you are in escrow and I really don't see just what businesses it is of yours anyway."

"Lady, your track record reads better than a checkout-stand novel. I can guess just exactly why your mother was asking you to come home."

"Oh, my mother wants me home all right, but I'm a little past the nest stage." But under her rules, and that wasn't likely to happen while Amber drew breath! The sheriff aimed hard black eyes at her again but Amber shook it off. There just wasn't any easy way to explain that your own, dear sweet mother was a witch. Most people just simply didn't have it in them to believe such a thing. Much less that a mother would cast something like a curse on her own offspring.

"It's not exactly a crime for a mother to be inviting her daughter home."

"That depends on the fine print." The man crossed his arms back over his chest in response. His arms bulged as he did it and Amber looked back over the demolished mess of her house. She wasn't crawling home just because a house was leveled. She hadn't even moved in yet anyway.

"I'll just have to find another place to live."

"I've got a guesthouse." Damn! Joe could have bitten his tongue off for letting those words slip out. The last thing he needed was this woman anywhere near him. Bad luck followed her like a trained pony. He had ten pages of car accidents, landslides, an earthquake and too many other catastrophes to name.

Little Red wasn't impressed anyway. She tossed a "get real" look at him before stomping away to her car. Watching her lean into the vehicle, Joe took a moment to admire her bottom again. Her stubborn streak rubbed at his anger as he stood looking at her and that car. There were long scratches on the door from her recent slide down an interstate hillside. Her house was a pile of scrap wood and she was being picky about his guesthouse?

"All right by me. But this isn't the only house that's been demolished. I'll have a new tenant in that guesthouse before nightfall." Joe slid his glasses back into place before giving her another long look with the mirrored finish to hide it. "But I thought you might like to consider that pet of yours. It's going to get cold tonight."

Flamingo? Oh...the man fought dirty! But he was right. Amber might not mind camping in her car for the sake of her pride. But tortoises didn't have pride, did they?

"How much is the rent?"

* * * * *

"Now don't look at me like that. Mama's found you a nice yard, hasn't she?" Flamingo gave another groan before the tortoise lumbered away and began eating the shrubbery that surrounded Amber's newest home.

Sheriff Lott's guesthouse was literally charming. It was also tiny. But it was just too cute for words and Amber loved it! Flamingo didn't seem too thrilled, but the tortoise would settle in.

The best part of the whole thing was the fact that the guesthouse sat almost half a mile from the sheriff's house. It wasn't so much a guesthouse as a mother-in-law house. That suited Amber just fine. It really wasn't anything personal but the sheriff just seemed to laugh at her a little too much. Add to that, the fact that he managed to show up at all of the wrong times lately... Well, he had solved the problem of just where Amber would be living.

So, for the next hour, she would be duty-bound to think good thoughts about the man. Tilting her head to the side, Amber considered Flamingo. Sheriff Lott had the best set of shoulders she'd seen in true living color.

Except that she'd hadn't really seen those shoulders in the flesh yet. Not that she was considering seeing the man without his shirt on, but there wasn't anything wrong with a little mental curiosity...

Oh, right.

Turning back towards her front door, Amber sent it closed with a shove. Maybe she did owe the man an hour of good thoughts, but her imagination didn't need to get so completely involved.

So, instead she'd go shopping! At the moment, the house was empty except for a cot that she'd had packed in her car. Considering the sleeping bag that had served as her bed for the past two weeks, Amber headed for the kitchen and her purse.

She was going shopping! Maybe she wouldn't have her insurance check for another week but that was why God had made credit cards.

* * * * *

"I quit."

The white enamel of Ken's teeth flashed through his lips before he answered. "You can't quit, it's against the rules of the bet. Uncle Tim was clear, loser is badge-boy for the two-year term." Ken tossed a handful of peanuts into his mouth and crushed them with a few strong motions of his jaw. "But you could always cry 'Uncle'. And welsh on the bet."

"Not in this lifetime." Joe glared at his sibling before making a grab for the peanut dish that had sat on his mother's coffee table for as long as he could remember. Ken tried to defend his claim on the bowl but came up too slow.

"Glad to hear it, Sheriff Lott. Nice badge, brother."

Joe dropped the snack dish and folded his fingers into a fist. There were just some things that adulthood couldn't change. Siblings, little brothers to be exact, would always need a good solid, right cross every now and again. It was an older brother's duty.

"Josiah Lott, you come in here and lend me a hand." Another thing time couldn't seem to touch was the way a mother could snap her child to attention despite the fact that he towered over her by eight inches. "Come on with you, leave your little brother alone."

Ken's face turned into a sharp frown. "Mom, we're the same size."

Deborah Lott leaned her head around the doorjamb and smiled at her sons. Sending her eldest a wink she went back to her kitchen as she sang out some country and western song about it wouldn't matter when he was eighty because he was always going to be her baby boy.

Leaning up against the kitchen counter, Joe eyed his mother. It absolutely amazed him, the complete control she managed to wield over her family. There was an infinite amount of strength compressed into her five and a half foot frame. Despite the gray that streaked her hair, she was the heart of the family. Sunday afternoon just wouldn't feel right if he wasn't spending it in his mom's kitchen.

"So, young man, tell your mother all about the nice girl you met this week."

Joe choked on the iced tea he'd tipped back. His mom immediately turned that knowing gleam of hers at him. "Don't know who you've been talking with, but I'm not remembering any girl that I met."

His mother turned away from the range and pegged him with her mother's eyes. "You don't need to imply that I'm some sort of busybody. Really, Bonnie Samson told me you lent out the cottage."

Little Red's face sprang up in his head in full color. So did the fact that he still thought she had one hell of a great backside. His mother continued to inspect his face with her razor-sharp eyes.

"Nothing personal, just business, Mom."

"What are you trying to pull over my eyes? Business? The property's been paid in full for ten years! You don't need a tenant."

"Especially this one." The words slipped out before Joe clamped his lips together. His mother gave a small huff before turning back to her culinary masterpiece.

"Then why on earth did you let someone move into the place?"

"Her house was totaled by Ruth and I felt sorry for her."

His mother lifted a lid and considered her work before slipping him a smile over her shoulder. "You're a fine man, Josiah. If I do say so myself."

Yeah. But he was sure a stupid one from time to time. Having Little Red bunking right down the road was setting his nerves on edge. He'd spent the last week working enough overtime to choke the image of her bottom out of his head.

So far, his strategy wasn't working too effectively.

The woman was just...well...sexy. To put it bluntly, she wiggled in all the places that made him sweat. Joe shifted as his jeans became uncomfortable. Little Red seemed to have found a quick start button on his sex drive. Thinking about her raised his flagpole now. Catching sight of her made his cock twitch.

But she had the temperament of a badger and the luck of the damned. Staying far away from Little Red was the wisest choice of action. His cock demanded the opposite as Joe shifted again and tried to resist the need to pull on the front of his pants in his mother's kitchen.

"You did remember to pull out the box of records from the bedroom closet?"

"Damn it!"

"Josiah! It's the Lord's day!" His mother propped a hand onto her hip and glared at him. "It's not all that big of a deal. Just give the girl a call and go and get the boxes. Painless as could be."

As painless as a root canal. His mom smiled as she considered the matter settled and turned back to her cooking. Joe let his eyes close in a moment of pure agony. It was a good thing they were going to services tonight. He was going to need the blessing to counterbalance his tenant's bad karma.

* * * * *

"It's absolutely perfect!" Amber considered her bed and smiled. All right, there wasn't a single other thing in the bedroom but the bed. Well, her bed was a work of artistic perfection. A feminine delight. Overindulgent to the extreme but hey, you only get to live once.

Besides, since she was renting, she'd have to contain her decorating ambitions. Amber loved to paint. Or wallpaper. In fact, her favorite Saturday morning necessity was making a trip to the local Home Depot.

Amber loved that store!

She turned away from the creamy, enameled walls of the bedroom as disappointment crushed her imagination. No possibilities here. But her bed was still perfection.

Queen-sized, quilt top with extra padding and just the most glorious comforter set she'd ever seen. Lavender and gold with lots of cream lace. Amber had bought every matching pillow they made and it was certainly worth the dent it made in her bank account.

The doorbell chimed for attention. Amber frowned but wandered into her tiny living room anyway. The deliverymen must have forgotten to get her signature or something. Her mattress set had only been dropped off in the last hour. The plastic packing material was still wadded up next to the door. Cutting the stuff up into small enough pieces to fit into her recycle bin was going to be a chore.

The bell rang again and Amber reached for the doorknob. Maybe she could sweet-talk the guys into taking the pile with them.

"Good evening." Little Red shrieked again. The front door slammed shut before she'd even finished her yelling. Joe let the door close. He'd like to plant his boot in the way again but he needed to stay on the woman's good side. At least long enough for him to get his mom's records.

The doorbell buzzed for attention again. Amber glared at the oak panel in front of her and groaned. She couldn't leave the man standing on her front porch. Pulling the door open she pinned a smile on her face.

"Good evening, Sheriff Lott." Amber felt her cheeks color with embarrassment. Being reduced to a shrieking female every time her landlord met her was really the pits. Considering the man in front of her, Amber took a closer look. Joe looked like he was on the way to jury duty. There was a resigned look sitting on his face as he stood watching her with his midnight eyes.

Amber felt her lips turn up into a smile. Somehow the idea that he was there, when he didn't want to be made it all so very amusing.

"What can I do for you?"

"My mother stored some boxes in the back closet."

"Oh, well, come in, I guess." It was a confusing invitation to issue. Amber considered Joe another second before she moved out of the doorway. Her amusement had suddenly vanished. Having the man inside the house was rather crowding. As small as the cottage was, it seemed to emphasize how big he was. There was a rush of sensation that moved over her skin as she considered his frame. The few men she knew just didn't make her feel small.

Joe did. She noticed things about him that she'd never really seen on other men. Her skin tingled as she actually caught and noticed what he smelled like. It was a warm scent that made her nipples tighten as that tingle zipped along her limbs and into her belly.

"What in blazes is that?"

Amber propped her hands onto her hips. "It's called a bed. All the civilized humans sleep in them these days."

Joe cocked his head around and let his teeth show. "There's so much estrogen leaking from that pile of satin and lace, I think you need to post a warning sign."

To hell with what her nipples thought! The man was a pig! "Excuse me, but I certainly don't need your approval on how my bedroom looks."

Joe looked over the lavender and green fluff again before looking back at Amber. Her face was flushed with anger and her body taut with it. Her nipples were hard little points that raised the fabric of her dress. The afternoon sun cut through her dress, displaying her body and every curve she had. His cock hardened instantly as he lingered over the curve of her hips.

"I didn't invite you in here, but I'll be delighted to toss you out!" Amber stretched her arm out and pointed at the door. Joe watched her breasts gently sway as she moved, and felt his mouth go dry. She stamped her foot and repeated her gesture. Arousal snaked up his spine as Joe considered Miss Amber Talisman. The woman was full of sass and it was giving him a hard-on from hell.

"So, what's wrong with me?" Joe watched her eyes widen at his question. The little blue orbs fluttered over his shoulders before she pushed her lips into a pout.

"What?" Amber glared at the man and stamped her foot again. Of all the nerve! She wanted him out! Now! His face was turned up in that half grin again as his eyes were sliding down her body. The smile on his face became infinitely deeper when he got back to looking at her face. Heat exploded in her face again. He was looking her over.

Of all the barbaric things to do! Sure, she had looked at his shoulders but that was just because he insisted on showing off by carrying Flamingo. That didn't give him the right to look at her nipples. His eyes dropped to the little telltale bumps showing through her dress and his lips pressed into a tight line. Amber felt her breath lodge in her throat as she watched the flare of desire brighten his eyes. Her nipples really liked the idea she saw crossing his face.

"You dog! Get out!"

Joe laughed. It was a low rumble that made her pick up one foot to move away from him before she thought about it. His dark eyes instantly caught the motion and Amber sent her foot back into the floor before she retreated. She wanted him gone—in fact, she needed him to go but she absolutely was not going to tuck tail and run. Her entire body was hot and every time his eyes moved down it she felt like his hands were there instead. Amber couldn't let that happen. Her heart tripled its pace as the very idea crossed her mind.

"You've probably got the right idea."

Amber sucked in a deep breath and felt her heart rate slowing down. Relief raced along her body just a second before she was hauled up against the solid form of Joe's body.

"But I like my ideas better." Placing his mouth over hers, Joe captured the shriek she let out. And then he took his time.

Chapter Four

He kissed her like a man. Amber clung to his shoulders. She suddenly understood that every other person who had ever kissed her had been a boy.

Joe didn't grab her. Instead he was molding her body to his. Their frames fusing together as desire raced along both their bodies. His touch was solid and steady as his hand moved down her back to the cheek of her bottom. Amber felt each finger as it curled around the curve of her bottom.

Her belly was pressed into the hard reality of his desire. His cock was stiff as he continued to probe her mouth with his tongue. His tongue traced her lower lip as pleasure rippled through her mouth, and as a little moan opened her jaw, Joe sent that hot tongue in towards her. The full taste of desire hit her as her belly quivered, and tempted her with the reminder of the hard cock pressing into her belly.

His hand kneaded her bottom as Amber felt the smooth slip of fluid from her body. Her passage clamored for attention as her hips gave a little jerk born from some deep instinct inside her womb.

Ripping her mouth away, Amber pushed against his chest. His arms fell open and she scrambled around the bed before facing off with him.

"No, no, no, no, no."

Little Red propped her hands on her hips but her lips were still shiny from his kiss. Joe let a smile lift his lips. Oh yes, she was full of sass. He couldn't decide if he wanted to kiss her some more or watch her throw a tantrum. Both ideas made him more determined to get back into contact with her body. The sparks lighting her eyes beckoned to him just as strongly as her little hard nipples did. The combination of fire and spunk fused into a driving force to conquer her objections. Maybe that was a primitive idea but Joe enjoyed the way it burned across his brain. Want didn't describe the feeling, this was need and it rode him hard.

"You can't do that to me." Amber glared at Joe as she forced her heart to slow down. All right! So the man could kiss! Big deal! She couldn't let it get to her. She didn't want a boyfriend and that was final.

"You mean kiss you? I just did." He moved with those long strides around her as his eyes watched the way she shifted in response. "You've got a sexy little bottom, Amber. I've wanted to touch it since I met you."

His deep voice washed over her and set off a reckless desire to let him do whatever he wanted with her. It struck her once again that Joe wasn't a boy. His dark eyes promised her a battle that her body leapt with delight over. If this man decided he wanted her, he would take her. "You can't just talk to me like that. You're the sheriff."

Joe reached one strong hand up and deliberately pulled on the collar of his shirt. He was wearing a burgundy button-front shirt today. It lay over the hard muscles of his chest far too nicely, reminding her that she'd had her fingertips resting on those shoulders and she'd wasted the chance to flatten her palms onto the hard strength that filled out that shirt.

"I'm off-duty and there's no law against a man telling a woman he likes what he sees."

He stepped closer and Amber felt her belly tighten instantly. One corner of his mouth lifted along with a dark eyebrow. "I liked what I tasted too, and so did you." His eyes darkened to midnight as he stepped closer and watched her reaction. "You kissed me back, honey, and I love that little tongue of yours."

Amber glared at him but what could she say? Well, there was one thing she could say.

"Get out of my bedroom!"

"Fine. I'm going." Joe pulled the box from the top of the closet before he turned towards the door. So much for being honest with a woman. All that got a guy was a temper tantrum.

"Red hair suits you." He turned at the door and looked at her bed. His black eyes made a slow investigation of it before slipping over her body once more. Amber felt her lungs seize as she very clearly read the message in those dark eyes.

"I guess I could get used to that bed after all."

* * * * *

Ah hell.

He shouldn't have done that. Joe had a list of chores a mile long and all he wanted to do was invent a few to do that included his guesthouse.

Well, he wasn't sorry. Little Red's lips were potent. He could still taste her an hour later. He was going to savor those lips the next time he got the chance to slide his own along them. He cast a long look at the guesthouse and grunted.

That chance wouldn't be arriving anytime soon. Little Red had turned the bolt the second he cleared the doorjamb. He took a moment to laugh over that immediate click his ears had noticed. She'd promptly stomped away into her kitchen too.

His little neighbor was just as affected as he was by that kiss. All amusement vanished as Joe considered the pulse rising along his bloodstream. He shouldn't have looked at that bed a second time. The image of her in those pajamas was giving him too much fuel for a mental picture of her lying bare among all that satin and lace.

Maybe there was nothing wrong with all that estrogen—his cock was twitching as testosterone filled his blood in response to her ultrafeminine bed.

Joe shook his head and went back into the yard. The gale-force winds had uprooted two of his trees and he had to get them cut down and hauled over to the curb for removal.

The work was hard and the sun beat down with unrelenting rays but there was satisfaction in the job. A man's property was worth the sweat of his labor.

Joe stopped and listened to the afternoon air. There was a distinct buzz hitting his ears. Moving down the length of land that separated the main house from the guest one, he tried to get a fix on where the sound was originating.

His cell phone chimed for attention and he pulled the thing off his belt. A line of numbers came across the digital screen making him grunt. So, much for a day off! Turning around, he headed for the house at a dead run.

* * * * *

"About time you got here."

Joe slipped into a dark apartment as the door was quickly closed behind him. The four men in the room were sitting amongst piles of video and sound surveillance equipment.

Pulling his glasses off, Joe scanned the monitors looking for the faces of his criminals. Pullman County was remote and its lack of sophistication had attracted the wrong sort of new resident.

Phil Dantrolp was known by a wide range of names and titles. Most referred to him as The Bear. What ticked Joe off was the fact that the drug dealer was currently walking around his town. His thousand-dollar linen suit stuck out at the local greasy spoon and his polished Spanish leather shoes didn't fit the working-class community.

The biggest dope problem his county had was the locals trying to grow their own stash of marijuana for their private consumption. Dantrolp dealt in more deadly forms of addiction. It was too much to hope that the recent hurricane would have sent the man and his business looking for some other town to pollute while making his transactions.

Instead, the monitor clearly showed him smoking a thin cigar as he leaned against a pillar next to the local mall. Moms with kids walked right by, and there currently wasn't a thing he could do about it. They needed evidence first. So far, the man was a master at getting out of convictions by lack of evidence.

That was why the FBI was sitting on stakeout at his local shopping center. It was the center of town. Right off the highway. Easy in, quick exit and a straight shot into Dallas.

"He's waiting for a drop, is my guess." Special Agent Krimmer looked over the rim of his glasses at the monitor. The man never took the shades off, instead he let them slide down his nose just enough to look over them. The man would jerk his head and send those shades back into place in a second. He stuck his thumb towards another set of monitors.

"Got a pair of traffickers hanging out in the parking lot with a backpack on one man. My guess is cocaine headed for Dallas. Now all we need is to get him with his hands on the product."

The communication line crackled as the field team reported in. Dantrolp chucked his cigar to the pavement a second later. He didn't bother to stomp his butt out. He turned and moved around the corner of the mall entrance. He slipped through a truck bay and the camera lost him.

"Shit!" Krimmer surged to his feet as he shouldered the door open. He sprinted around the corner as Joe charged after him. The mall passed in a blur as they took the truck bay in two long strides.

"Pleasure doing business with you." The words floated through a fence but it was one of those chain link ones with slats of solid wood sent down the links to give more privacy. All Joe saw was a jumble of puzzle images. He hit the fence still running and pushed his body right over the top of it.

Gravity slammed him back to earth as he landed on steady feet. A flurry of motion met his eyes as one of the men took a swing at him. Deflecting the blow and securing the suspect took only a minute but the chase had moved on without him. Joe ground his teeth together as he hooked his suspect by the biceps and propelled him after the rest of Krimmer's team. That's the thanks he got for being faster. Left behind with the first catch of the day.

The excitement was over. The other two suspects were cuffed and backed against a wall. The smirk sitting on Dantrolp's face made Joe cuss.

Krimmer joined him. "He dumped the evidence."

Joe looked back along the truck loading bay they were in. Nothing was on the pavement. He looked at the semi-solid chain link fence.

The bastard had tossed his load into the parking lot. It was public enough to shed reasonable doubt on the case.

The radio crackled to life. "We got it and a witness."

Dantrolp cussed this time. Krimmer's eyes almost glowed over the rim of his shades.

* * * * *

A witness.

Those were sweet, sweet words. Joe turned around the end of that fence and smiled as he looked at the best damn luck he'd had all month.

"Get your paws off me, mister."

Holy Christ in heaven! Joe stared and tried to make the image fade. Instead, Amber propped her hands on her hips and shot Krimmer's teammates a scathing look.

The backpack was lying at her feet. White powder decorated her black top like powered sugar. The stuff was even in her hair. Dantrolp had slung the thing over the fence and hit her with it.

No one could possibly have that bad of luck...except his Little Red.

"Ma'am, we need your statement."

"That doesn't include touching me." Amber glared at her tormentor again before taking a swipe at her clothing. She was a mess.

Her wrists were grabbed before she'd finished swiping over her breasts.

"Hey!" The grip was solid steel and she lifted her face to stare into a pair of familiar black eyes. "Let me go." Her voice lacked the firm authority she'd had just seconds before. She snorted under her breath as she tried to jerk away from Joe.

"That's evidence, Amber. Leave it alone until we get you something else to wear."

A camera appeared and began taking shots of the backpack that had landed on her. The thing had split open and dumped its white powder all over the place. Her head throbbed from the collision.

"I'm not pressing charges against the guy."

"No, I am." Joe let her hands go slowly. He enjoyed the feel of her soft skin. The simple contact brought their morning encounter to immediate recall in his brain.

"No statement!" No way! Amanda stepped away from the continuing photo shoot as she glared at Joe. His face had gone solid as stone at her words. A stupid lump on her head wasn't worth getting subpoenaed to court over.

"Just let the guy go with a warning to save his dunk shots for the basketball court." The guy in question sent her a smirk. Amber glared at the polished exterior he presented along with his casual attitude. You'd think she might have earned a thank you for not hauling him into civil court. Joe glared right back at him. In fact, Amber found the urge to move back pestering her brain.

"You two have issues," she announced after watching their mental battle as it continued.

"Yeah, I've got a thing for out-of-town scum messing up *my* town."

The tone of his voice suddenly made Amber take a second look at the scene. The two guys were actually handcuffed and being guarded by two other large men. One man looked at her through his shades as he directed the photographer around the area with silent hand gestures. Joe looked like he was standing within arm's reach of her on purpose.

Her head was shaking back and forth as she refused to accept that the situation was some sort of crime scene. She looked at her feet at the backpack. The white powder was spilling out of plain zip-lock bags, not a package of powdered sugar as she'd assumed.

A camera flashed in her face, making her jump. It just couldn't be. Amber looked at her hands and the white residue coating her fingers. She lifted her hand to her face and sniffed her fingers. No sweet smell of sugar filled her senses. Instead another flash made her vision sparkle.

"Oh Jesus!" She ripped the loose top over her head and flung it away from her body. The cameraman jumped as her top went sailing over his shoulder.

That was Little Red for you. Joe watched her shake her head like a dog after a bath. She shook her hands so hard her wrists popped. And her breasts bounced in the lace cups of her bra making him shift as he was torn between the need to laugh and the urge to groan.

His Little Red had just the right mixture of curves and spunk. Joe suddenly noticed that Krimmer was taking notice of the same things he was. He yanked his jacket off and took one long step towards Amber.

She shrieked but the jacket muffled the sound. Solid steel arms bound the nylon windbreaker around her. Amber hissed and struggled to free a hand to wipe her hair out of her face. The hard, muscled arms of the local sheriff prevented even a finger from escaping. She flipped her neck up and glared at the man.

She shouldn't have done that. He was far too hunky for close quarters. Her eyes lingered on those firm male lips and the recent memory of them sliding over hers. Oh yeah…way too close for comfort.

"I've got it. Thanks."

Joe let her go and held the corners of his lips down as they tried to twitch up. Her little blue eyes had practically devoured his mouth. The look went straight to his head and sent his blood racing south.

The timing lacked a whole hell of a lot. He was going to have to remember to investigate Little Red's effect on him before their encounters became too public.

Joe grunted under his breath as he considered that idea. He didn't need the hassle. He looked at the white mess covering her red hair and shook his head. His body had clear objections to his logic. His brain might be telling him to hightail it as far away from Red as his legs could carry him but deep down in the center of that same brain was the rising heat of need.

Her blue eyes blinked as she considered the clear message crossing his. The tip of her little pink tongue appeared and traced her lower lip as she stepped away from what she saw. Joe let his lips curl up into a grin as he watched her.

"I am moving to Idaho." Amber eyed his badge as she announced her plan of escape. Joe lifted an eyebrow at her.

"Doesn't it snow there?"

"I could learn to like snow. I might have real talent in the snowman-building department." Amber didn't try to understand where his comment might lead. He was a man and therefore completely illogical. Testosterone brain-damaged from birth. Doomed to annoy the female population until death.

"And what will Flamingo do?"

* * * * *

Joe shouldn't be able to use her pet against her. Amber snorted and hissed as she stood under the showerhead. She'd already used half a bottle of shampoo but she turned the bottle over and filled her hand again.

Cocaine! Her hair was never going to be clean again. She'd have rather been doused with a bag of live fleas. Drug dogs could smell the stuff on luggage that had just been transported next to a bag with the drug in it. She was going to get eaten the next time she went near an airport.

But Joe was right, she couldn't move to Idaho.

Joe? Exactly when had she started thinking about him as Joe? Her memory decided to remind her of how well the man kissed. It had curled her toes and sent her body into heatstroke. Even standing under hot water she felt her cheeks flush.

Sometimes, she detested her gender.

"Are you ever coming out of there?"

A handful of water came sailing over the top of the shower door. Joe jumped back through the doorway as it hit him square in the face.

"And stay out!"

She had to come out sometime. Joe looked at his watch and waited. Amber wouldn't have any skin left if she didn't emerge soon. The door to the department locker room opened barely a foot as she poked her head out to peer into the hallway.

"Ready?"

His deep voice sounded far too amused. Amber considered asking him why but looked down the hallway again instead. She had other worries at the moment.

"Do you have any of those drug dogs around here?"

"We have two in the county but they aren't in the station. Why?"

Little Red tossed her head and pushed the door open. Her hair was still wet and didn't flip out of her face as she'd wanted. One arm rose as she used a hand to push the dark strands behind her ear.

"Let's just say I don't want to test how keen their sense of smell is."

"Considering your luck, I wouldn't want to risk their incisors either."

She propped her hands onto her hips and thrust those plump breasts forward. Her lips twisted into a pout as Joe let a little smile of amusement lift his lips.

"That is not funny." Well, it was sort of amusing, in a hysterical kind of way. But that didn't mean anyone was allowed to laugh about it except for her. His eyebrow lifted before Joe pushed away from the wall he was leaning against. Amber tried to pull her eyes away from the man's chest but they lingered over the hard muscles she knew lay under that shirt. Heat exploded in her face as she caught his eyes watching her. All amusement faded from his expression as his eyes became twin flames.

"Come on, we'd better take care of business." Joe's eyes made another pass over her chest before sending a promise back at her face. "Before we get too distracted."

"I am not distracted."

A low rumble of male amusement shook his chest as Joe stepped towards her, and Amber felt her nipples begin to tighten again. "No, honey, you are distracting."

Amber gasped and shot off towards his office. Joe followed behind her and enjoyed the sway of her hips. It was possible that he'd finally tumbled into insanity but at the moment he was enjoying it too much to really care. All he wanted to do was get the excuse to investigate the way Amber felt next to him. But more importantly, he couldn't wait to listen to the way she whimpered when he kissed her.

Amber should have been grateful for the chore of writing down her statement. Instead it was an endless event that she struggled to endure. All she wanted to do was look over the stunning example of manhood that sat across the desk from her. Her blood raced through her veins as her skin turned hot and she tried to keep her eyes on the paper in front of her.

Her libido had lousy timing and bad aim. There were plenty of targets she could think of to get excited over that wouldn't be so...ah...overpowering. Her eyes kept peeking through her lashes at the wide shoulders her fantasies insisted on lingering over.

For that matter, the man just might be married. Amber let her eyes travel over his left hand. Joe was typing away at a computer keyboard and his attention was on the screen. Sure, he'd kissed her but that didn't mean he wasn't a dog.

Something inside her cringed at that idea. Joe wasn't a cheating husband. She just knew he wasn't that kind of man. That didn't mean he didn't have a girlfriend. Some men didn't consider having two girlfriends as cheating. They thought it meant they were well-seasoned. It was really funny how that same rule never applied to women. Two boyfriends meant you were easy pickings.

His left hand landed on the center of the desk. The fingers spread out wide. He left it exactly like that before turning his dark eyes away from the computer screen and onto her.

"I'm not married. No ex-wife and no girlfriend. No kids that anyone ever told me about either, but I like them."

Amber tried to shrug it off. Nope, she wasn't feeling anything in connection to his announcement. The warm flush bleeding down her spine was just relief that the report appeared to be finished.

His eyes sharpened and traced the blush on her cheeks before they moved over her mouth. A tingle of fear followed that heat down her back as Joe aim a clear promise back into her eyes. Determination blazed across the desk as she tossed her head but the man in front of her only frowned. A single nod of his head made her eyes widen.

"We'll see about that later, Amber."

"Oh no, we won't." Amber was on her feet before the last word left her mouth. Joe moved with amazing speed. That innocent-looking hand snaked forward and caught her wrist in an iron grasp. His thumb gently stroked the delicate skin of her inner wrist as he held her in place. Her body jumped in response as sensation rushed towards her belly and heat ignited inside her passage. The dark promise blazing from his eyes made her lips tingle with anticipation.

"I think we will." Joe stood up. Her blue eyes widened again as she shivered. The little quiver ran the length of her arm before it traveled along her body. Her little nipples would be hard. Joe knew it and cursed the bulky jacket he'd found her to wear. He wanted to see the two little nubs pushing against her clothing to declare her response to him.

Instead she gave a yank on her arm and he let her wrist go.

"Thank you, Ms. Talisman, I'll be in touch."

She ran out of his office. Joe laughed. It wasn't the sound of amusement though. Instead it was a deep rumble of promise that shook his chest. He could almost smell her in the air that lingered around his desk. His blood was racing through his veins as his cock itched to be free. Hell, it wanted a whole lot more, but Amber wasn't done running yet.

Yeah, he'd be in touch.

Chapter Five

Amber grinned and then giggled. She stepped back to look at her newest creation and purred with delight.

"That ought to suit Joe."

She placed her vase of silk flowers in the corner of her room. The one you saw as you entered the bedroom. It was a two-foot tall, cream-colored vase that was round and plump. She arranged the silk flowers just right. The entire arrangement was almost four feet high when you included the vase. But with nothing else in the room besides the bed it looked delightful.

Like something from a *County Living* magazine. And the best part was…it leaked estrogen!

Sunlight streamed through the windows as she ran a hand over her brow. It was warm today. A thump and scratch at the door made her smile. Flamingo wanted some attention.

Picking up a paperback book, she took a second to pour herself a glass of iced tea before heading out her side door. Flamingo was at the back one. If she opened it the tortoise would try to get into the house, and considering how big her pet had gotten, Flamingo would most likely win.

"Hi, baby, Mama heard you." Amber sat down on a patio chair near the fence. There was just enough shade to cover her head and shoulders. She stretched her legs out into the sun for a little tanning time. Her pet slowly turned away from the door and lumbered over to nuzzle Amber's ankles.

The afternoon was perfect. A little breeze and the sun wasn't too hot either. There was even the buzzing of bees in the air. Amber smiled as she opened her book and tried to pick up the story.

A loud thump from her front door interrupted her. There was only one person who would knock on her door. She considered getting up to open the door and decided to stay put. Maybe Joe would go away. Or maybe he'd just walk around the house. But somehow, that felt like a safer bet than inviting the man back into her house.

"I know you're home, Amber."

Amber groaned and bent the corner of the page on her book. No garage meant her car was in the driveway.

"I'm out in the back."

Joe appeared almost immediately. Amber felt her nerve endings contract as she took in the civilian clothing he was wearing. She'd been ignoring that last promise he'd shot her all day. Trying to convince herself that the man had merely been flirting and it would never amount to anything else.

Flamingo hissed as his long legs stepped into the tortoise's vision. Joe halted as his dark eyes inspected the reptile. Amber grinned and gave her pet a loving pat. Flamingo immediately stretched his neck out for a scratch as well.

"That animal is actually affectionate?"

"Yes, and loyal as well as possessive of me."

Joe watched as Amber scratched the neck on her pet and then the tortoise moved its head until that hand was scratching the opposite side of its neck.

The tortoise lost his attention as he noticed the bare legs stretched out in the afternoon sunlight. Long, firm legs that made his mouth water. Even her feet were bare. The little toenails painted red.

"I brought you a list of my private contact numbers." He handed a small, neatly printed list to her. Amber continued to scratch her pet. Having the animal between her and Joe was very soothing.

"Why would I need those?"

Joe grinned and leaned forward until he grasped her hand off Flamingo's head. He pressed the paper into her hand and curled her fingers around it with his larger hand. The skin to skin contact burned as his eyes caught hers with firm authority.

"You're a witness. But if anyone in this county needed those numbers, I figured it would be you."

Amber jerked her hand free and scowled at him. "Gee, thanks."

"Don't mention it."

He was right. Amber didn't like it but she really should have the contact information. You never knew when life was going to throw you a curveball.

Joe caught the acceptance on her face and gave a brief nod of his head. He swung his eyes around to consider the patio. He seemed to systematically look over every plank in the fence, judging it for security. The way he stood and moved suddenly hit her on a deeper level. It felt almost like she trusted his ability to protect her, but there was something polished about his movements. It wasn't the normal cop training. It just hinted at a man who was far more deadly when he needed to be.

It was an odd concept but deeply rooted inside her brain and Amber wasn't laughing. Instead her eyes slipped over his shoulders and down his narrow waist and over his jeans-clad legs. Strength was etched into each and every curve that denim showed her.

He nodded approval at the fence before tipping his head back towards her. His eyes caught the basketball near her feet and he'd scooped it up before Amber surged up from her seat.

"No! Don't touch the ball!!"

Her warning was too late. Flamingo hissed and sent all of his hundred and fifty pounds into Joe's legs. He stumbled off balance and sent a hand towards the trunk of a tree to break his fall.

The gentle buzzing of the bees suddenly rose to a deafening level as Joe's entire frame hit the young tree and it shook violently under the impact. A black cloud rose around the top of it as the buzzing became hostile.

"Oh, shit!"

Joe hooked her arm and sent her crashing into the back door. Amber frantically tried to turn the doorknob as Joe's body landed right on top of hers. The door swung inwards and they fell into the house in a jumble of limbs. Joe lifted her out of her tracks and sent her spinning across the tile floor as he slammed the door shut so hard the windows rattled.

"Holy crap!" Joe grabbed a dishtowel and swiped at the few bees that had made it into the house. "Are there any windows open?"

"No," Amber yelped as one bee found a target on her thigh. Her skin screamed as Joe sent the towel whizzing towards the insect. It popped off her leg and he crushed it beneath the heel of his boot. She looked at the pane of glass set in the center of the door. The patio was engulfed in a swarm of angry bees.

Flamingo had pulled his body into his shell and the insects continued to look for a target for their venom.

"Are you allergic to bees?" Joe was almost afraid to ask the question. Her thigh was turning bright red as a welt the size of a quarter appeared. He lifted her off her feet and sat her on the counter as he looked at the wound. The little black stinger was still visible.

"Hold still."

"No! Don't pull it out."

With one hand holding her thigh in place, Joe looked up with a harassed look on his face. "Why not? It needs to come out."

"I know, but plucking will break the venom sacks attached to it. Hand me my purse."

Her handbag landed in her lap but his hand never released her thigh. The burn of the sting was making her eyes glassy with unshed tears. Amber pulled her ATM card out and used it to slide the stinger out of its target.

"See? Newest mom trick. I saw it on the morning news a while ago."

"Great, you can get the ones on my back."

His shirt went over his head in a blur before he turned and backed right up to her. His body went right between her spread thighs. His shoulders didn't stop until he was just inches from her chest.

Oh yeah, he qualified for the title of hunk. Under that shirt was a chest that was sculpted to perfection. The muscles packed onto his wide shoulders and tapered away to a narrow and very tight waist. Joe defined sexy. Her mouth went dry and her nipples hard.

"You didn't answer my question. Are you allergic to bee stings?"

"No. At least I never have been before."

Amber tried to tear her eyes off his skin and direct her attention to the task at hand. Two spots were turning red on one shoulder blade. Only the size of nickels but the stingers still needed to come out. She laid a hand over the skin to smooth it flat. Her fingers immediately rejoiced in the feel of his warm flesh. The insane urge to run those fingers across the width of his frame made her shiver.

Lying naked next to this man must be mind-blowing.

Oh Lord, Amber! Shut up!

Two steady motions of her hand and the stingers came free. Joe moved away and shrugged back into his shirt while she tried to contain her whimper.

Joe didn't miss the look on her face. His cock stiffened immediately. Hell, like he wouldn't get a hard-on standing between those thighs! Just a little pair of shorts separated him from her center. He turned and walked towards the back door again. The bees were still swarming.

"Where is your phone?"

"Ah…"

The sound wasn't promising. Joe looked at Amber as she jumped down from the counter and pointed out onto the patio.

"You don't have a house phone? I know the line is active."

"Hey, it's on the shopping list but my insurance hasn't paid up yet. So, I was making do with my cell for now."

And it was sitting next to her book on the chair with the angry bees. "Don't you have a cell phone?"

He reached for his waist and cussed in the same moment. Looking out of the window, he found his phone lying at the base of the tree. The impact must have unhooked it from his waistband.

They watched the swarming insects as they buzzed around Flamingo's shell.

"What about the front door?"

"Those are killer bees, my darling, they'll be on me before I hit my yard." Joe snorted before turning around to glare at his company. "Explain to me why that animal of yours rammed my leg?"

"You touched the basketball."

"Yeah, and what? Flamingo doesn't like to share his ball? Let me guess, he's got a great hook shot?"

"Well…" Amber hesitated and moved away from him before giving in to the urge to giggle. "See, due to a lack of options, Flamingo thinks the basketball is…well…cute."

He rubbed his forehead before looking at her with complete disgust.

"Your tortoise has a blowup girlfriend?"

Amber nodded as Joe glared at her. "Tell me why you named that animal Flamingo?"

"Giant tortoises are hard to accurately sex when they're young and he'd already learned his name by the time certain…hmm…*things* developed."

Joe walked to the sink and flipped the hot water on. He scrubbed his hands as well as any surgeon getting ready for the operating room. Steam rose up as he turned the dishwashing liquid bottle over his hands and coated them with the antibacterial soap.

Her face was turning pink as she tried to stifle her giggles. But her little nipples were hard enough to cut glass. Joe looked at the plump swell of her breasts as he realized they were stuck together for the next few hours. Killer bees didn't give up easily.

She sobered instantly. The look in his eyes went straight to her belly. She was suddenly hot and achy. Her eyes slipped down his body until they found the unmistakable bulge of his crotch. The fabric was being pushed out by swelling that she suddenly wanted to release for him.

"This isn't right!"

Her announcement made him angry. His lips curled back to flash his teeth at her before he moved in that lightning fast way again. His arm clasped her to his body as his hand found the cheek of her bottom and firmly pressed her to the bulging crotch.

"Why not? Do you have a boyfriend?"

"No."

She wiggled but froze when a low groan came out of his chest. His eyes were twin flames that blazed their path to hers. His free hand gently stroked the skin on her neck, making her shiver. He kept going until his thumb covered the tight little button of her nipple. He pressed and circled the swollen tip making pleasure zip down her body and back up again.

"It looks pretty right to me."

She opened her mouth to protest. Joe caught those lips before they let a single word out. The sweet taste of her mouth made him desperate for her. The little nipple in his hand begged for attention as he sent his tongue deeply into her mouth to mingle with her own. A little moan of rapture escaped her throat as she let the velvet tip of her tongue stroke the length of his.

She had to be allergic to the bee strings. Nothing else explained the fever. Amber was so hot and found her body twisting against his. She wanted to be closer. Needed to feel that hard chest against her aching breasts. The smell from his skin was intoxicating.

His hands controlled her body with amazing strength. He sent his tongue deeply into her mouth as he gripped the back of her head. Stabbing into her mouth, he explored it in detail as her tongue twisted and stroked the length of his.

Heat ran down her body in rivers. The walls of her passage became enflamed as she felt the slide of fluid down their sides. It was such a primitive reaction. She twisted against his hold but couldn't stop her thoughts from desiring the same type of penetration for her body as his mouth was taking from hers.

Nothing seemed to matter but the pure need coursing through her blood. His hand moved to her waist and lifted her from the floor. Their lips parted but he ran his down the column of her neck as he turned and lowered her to the kitchen counter.

His fingers found the bottom of her T-shirt and pulled the garment up over her head.

"You have no idea what looking at these yesterday did to me." His voice was thick and husky. She'd never heard that tone used in response to her body before. It made her feel so beautiful. His eyes moved over her breasts with absolute devotion. His fingers brushed the top of them right before the lace-edged cups of her bra ended. A shiver shook her body as her blood raced through her veins too fast to understand. Her nipples tightened painfully as they begged to be introduced to his hot mouth.

"Show them to me."

His voice was rough but hard. His eyes flashed to her as his hands lingered over her rib cage. "Show me those little nipples that get hard every time we meet."

His demand made her tremble. Somehow, the idea that he wanted her to obey him made it so much more intense.

The little clasp that held her bra shut was in front. Amber forced her fingers to snap the thing open. His eyes didn't drop to her chest. Instead they watched hers as she fed her need to be bare in front of him.

Her eyes didn't tell him to stop. Joe watched the way she struggled with the idea. Indecision was written on her face even as her cheeks were covered with a blush. His body surged forward with the need to taste her. Her feminine scent rose from her spread thighs making his cock pulse with hunger. It was the sharp bite of need that made his teeth clench when a small click told him she'd opened her bra for him.

"Good girl." His voice whispered just one inch from her ear. His teeth nipped the lobe as his fingers smoothed over her shoulders. The straps slid down her arms until he tossed the garment onto the counter.

Two hands gently cupped her breasts making her moan. But he didn't look yet. Instead his face returned to hers as his fingers softly rubbed the globes of flesh. His lips hovered only an inch from hers making her yearn for another of his hot kisses.

"Kiss me."

He laughed at her request. Rich male amusement that made his chest vibrate. His mouth captured hers a second later. This time it was slow and hot. His tongue traced the surface of her lower lip before seeking out the length of her own.

Her hips twitched forward out of pure need. Her passage was so wet for him. Somewhere in the back of her skull was the nagging idea that she should use her common sense and stop. But her nipples screamed louder for the hot lips that were on hers. The walls of her passage contracted as they tried to condense the empty space inside them. She felt so much. Every finger on each of his hands as he gently lifted each of her breasts.

"What color are your nipples?"

"Huh?" Why didn't he just look? Waiting was driving her crazy. Need burned through the little hard tips making her moan from sheer sensation.

Joe let that little rumble of amusement shake his chest again. Her eyes were wide as they stared into his. The hot smell of need came from her body making him sweat as he held on to his control. Women were amazing creatures. Any man lucky enough to get naked with one should take his time.

"I want you to tell me what color these…" his thumbs flicked over the hard points of her breasts, "…delightfully hard nipples are."

She didn't understand why he needed her to tell him. But the idea made her shiver again.

"Are you one of those dominant kind of guys?"

A grin appeared on his face. "Are you a submissive kind of girl?"

She never had been but an image formed in her head of him making her submit to him. Kneeling in front of his body and taking the erection that was pushing his jeans out in her mouth at his command.

His grin was getting bigger as he watched her face. His thumbs flickered across her nipples again but he still didn't look at them. "I'm not some boy who thinks the best part of sex is the fucking. I don't get my kicks out of pain either. But a little command and compliance can be fun."

"I didn't agree to have sex with you." The words startled her. Her breasts were bare and her thighs spread open as his hips stood between them. His body was so strong and hers so hot. She wasn't thinking at all.

She should be. His hands moved on her breasts again but didn't touch her aching nipples. Instead he circled around them, never moving over them to give her what she wanted. His eyes were hard as he stared into hers.

"Let's get one thing clear, honey, I don't play prom night games. Either you're woman enough to deal with a man or go run back home to your mama." His thumbs found her nipples and flicked over them. Desire flamed bright and true in her eyes. Joe clenched his teeth together and refused to dip his head towards those hard nubs.

She was going to have to tell him. The skin on his face was drawn tight but control appeared to be woven into the very cells of his body. She'd insulted his pride and the price was going to be her relenting. That or letting her body burn from the inside out because she wouldn't tell him what he wanted. Maybe he had a point. She wasn't a girl anymore. To have sex or not was her choice.

"They're coral."

Coral. The knowledge undid him. Need surged through his hold on his imagination. Her breasts were perfect in his hands. Heavy and soft but the nipples were hard enough to cut a mirror. His cock jerked and pressed against his fly.

Goddamn it! Coral nipples and red hair.

Temptation called him towards the promise his fingers told him he'd find on top of those plump mounds.

Amber gasped. She listened to the sound of her own cry and almost didn't believe that sound had come from her. His mouth scorched her nipple. Hot and wet, his lips closed over the point as his tongue lapped the aching nub. Her fingers curled into the fabric of his shirt as her back arched to offer her breast completely to his attention.

Her hips demanded she move them. Small little jerks that just seemed necessary as he sucked harder on her nipple. Her passage clenched as more fluid flooded the channel. Sex had never been so intense before. Her body had never demanded it so loudly that not a single other idea even entered her brain.

All she thought about was those hot lips pulling on that nipple and the fact that its twin screamed for its turn.

"God, you're sweet. So damn sweet."

Joe found her opposite nipple and gently ran the tip of his tongue around it. She was perfect. Her skin smelled so fresh, the scent seemed to urge him forward towards the deepest touch male and female could share. He could smell the flow from her body. He knew she was wet for him. He captured the nipple between his lips and sucked it into his mouth. The little cry that came from her throat made him growl around his treat.

"Take your shirt off." Amber was desperate to get rid of the fabric between her fingers and his shoulders. Her mind was full of that brief image she had of those powerful arms. She needed to touch him. Get closer to the hard strength of his body.

His mouth left her breast. A little whimper caught in her throat but it emerged as a purr when he ripped his shirt over his head. The way his arms moved fascinated her. So much strength. It hit her as extremely male. As though she was noticing the difference in their genders for the first time in her life.

Joe forced his body to stand in place. Her blue eyes roamed over his chest like little beams of heat. Stroking and touching him despite the distance between them. The look on her face almost humbled him. Her eyes were full of admiration for him. It went beyond lust somehow. Her nude torso was thrust forward with hard nipples that begged for more attention. She had her hands flattened on the countertop to support her arched back. Her thighs were spread open and stayed there as she looked over his bare chest. A woman who wanted you was beautiful, one that needed you was stunning.

His cock twitched and he suddenly had to see the rest of her. The little pair of shorts made him angry as they prevented him from seeing her completely.

His face became harsh. Amber felt her eyes go large as he reached for her. His grip was firm but not biting. He lifted her from her perch as one hand caught the waistband of her last garment and pulled it from her body. Cool air hit her fevered skin making her sigh. But the harsh look on his face made her tremble. He wanted to take her. In the most primitive of a manners. Spread her body open as he penetrated deeply into her most secret place.

Excitement poured over her in response yet she shivered again as she felt the sheer power of that body. She craved his strength yet embraced how superior his body was to hers.

Her skin hit his making him grunt. Need was becoming too powerful to control. Her heavy feminine scent was overpowering every civilized cell in his brain. Needs that had never surfaced before sailed into his brain as he caught her mouth in a hard kiss of ownership. He thrust deeply into her body and grunted approval as she gently sucked on his tongue.

"I want to look at you." His voice was harsh. She landed gently on the counter again as he backed away from her body. She was completely vulnerable to his eyes. They traced every curve until they dropped to the center of her spread thighs.

She shivered but watched his harsh features. There was something so primitive about his viewing her. Almost like he was inspecting her before granting her his body to mate with. The pure magnificence of his bare chest made her hold her body still for those sharp eyes.

She was more than wet for him. The little curls over her mons glistened in welcome. Her hips twitched forward as need burned along her body. His was erupting into action at the sight of her spread body. She wanted him, it was written on her face.

She should be thinking. Amber tried to engage her brain. Instead Joe dropped a hand to his fly and her body took complete control. He popped the button fly open with sharp motions. The heavy rod of his cock fell through the opening making her gasp. It was swollen and red, looking too large to fit inside her. But her passage screamed for it to stretch her to accommodate him.

His hands caught her hips as the hard head of that cock nudged the folds of her sex open. His lips found her ear as he cooed softly and pressed forwards.

"Hold on to me, honey."

Her hands found his shoulders and rejoiced as her palms flattened on top of his skin. He pressed into her body and stretched her passage with his length. Pain and pleasure mixed inside her as he pulled back and thrust forward again. His hands held her firmly in place as he bucked between her legs and penetrated further.

"Oh yes!" The words were born from need. Amber had never wanted anything so much. She craved more but his hand held her exactly in place.

"Easy, baby." His voice was thick and harsh as his fingers pressed into her skin. A deep breath expanded his chest as he moved between her thighs with a slow thrust. He pulled free and her hips tried to follow but his hands held her still. His face lifted and his eyes aimed their sharp command at hers again. "Nice and easy, baby. Slow and steady." Amber didn't have any choice but to obey, he held her bottom in place as his hips thrust his cock back into her body.

She was too damn tight. Joe ground his teeth together as the urge to pound into her rode him hard. The little sounds of pleasure from her throat didn't help. Instead they pressed him on to complete loss of control. All he wanted to do was fuck. Hard and deep until her body gripped and milked him dry.

The cheeks of her bottom filled his hands as he thrust forward. She stretched and shivered until he felt the last inch of his cock bury itself inside her. Sweat beaded on his brow as he held steady and let her body adjust. He could feel the swollen nub at the top of her sex against his cock. Pulling out, he made sure to slide the entire length of his cock along that little button.

"Oh my God!" Amber jerked and dug her fingernails into his shoulders. No one had ever done that! Pleasure spiked through her until she panted. He thrust back into her and she almost screamed for mercy. It was too intense. The pleasure tightening and twisting her until she didn't know what to do. His hands wouldn't let her do anything. They held her still as he thrust into her body, his hips flexing back and forth between her thighs. He made sure to draw the length of his cock along her slick folds each and every time. She couldn't control the pleasure as it burst into a storm of heat that burned her body in a single flame of explosion.

"That's it, isn't it, baby?" She whimpered as Joe made sure to make his next thrust slow and hard. Her fingernails cut into his shoulder and the little pain made him hungry for more. The tight body wrapped around his cock drove him towards the insane desire to slam into her, but the sweet moan rising from her throat made him thrust his cock back into her with a slow motion that stroked her little clit.

"Look at me, Amber."

His voice was hard with authority. Amber didn't care. She lifted her eyelids to stare into the hard probe of his eyes as his body pulled free from hers. His face was drawn tight as he thrust deeply into her again. All the pleasure was twisting into a knot that was so intense it almost felt like pain.

"I want to watch you come." Her thighs tightened on his hips as his words hit her. Defiance flashed briefly across her face before he pulled his cock along her clit once again.

She moaned with rapture, making him grin. His cock needed the same release but the need to watch her climax burned in his brain. He slammed his length deep into her body as the walls of her passage gripped him. Her nipples stabbed into his chest as her fingernails cut into his shoulders. He rode her through the pleasure as her eyes dilated and his cock burned with the need to join her. Her body flooded with her release and Joe felt his control shred. He jerked and thrust deeply into her body. His hands held her bottom in place as he bucked and thrust hard.

His seed hit the deepest center of her body as she tightened around him and pulled, making him groan as pleasure erupted along every nerve ending he had, but it all centered around the hot flesh gripping his cock. Her body milked him as her head fell to his shoulder.

Pleasure pulsed from their connected bodies as Joe listened to the little whimpers coming from his partner. Her passage still clung to his cock as her hips pressed forward for the last drop of his seed. The smell of her skin hit his senses as the most feminine scent he'd ever encountered. His hands gently stroked the smooth length of her back as his cock twitched with the remains of climax.

* * * * *

The bees were settling down. Joe looked out the kitchen window and wished the damn insects had more of a temper. Amber's nipples stabbed into his chest and he was still buried inside her wet body. All he wanted to do was take her into that ultrafeminine bedroom for the rest of the day.

He had to let her go though. Reality was arriving as both their bodies became sated. She wiggled in his embrace. The clawing hands became gentle pushes for release. She ducked her head as he stepped back and jumped lightly to her feet. That sassy bottom flashed by as she went scurrying after her discarded clothing.

Ah, hell.

He hadn't planned it but the plain truth was, he wasn't sorry. Not in the least. No one could predict just when the blood would rise in response to another person. Men were a little more accepting of that fact. Little Red was nervous. He wasn't exactly sure what to make of their combustive effect on each other.

But he did know, he wasn't going to ignore it.

She really needed a shower. Oh God! She'd done some impulsive things in her life but never had she had wild sex! Everything was backwards! You went to dinner with a nice guy. Then maybe a kiss to see if there was any heat. After you checked around and made sure he wasn't a cheating dog or a deadbeat father, or on probation, you let him take you out again.

People did not have sex on kitchen counters! At least not normal kinds of people like her.

"Are you all right, Amber?"

"Fine." Her voice squealed as she wrapped her arms over her breasts.

"Uh-huh."

He raised an eyebrow at her while pulling his shirt back into place. Why did he get to look so composed? That wasn't fair! He turned to look out the window at their venom-wielding captors.

"Grab your purse, I think we can make it to your car now."

"Help yourself, I'll just wait for the beekeeper to show up."

He chuckled at her and turned those sharp eyes back to inspect her face.

"I'm contacting an exterminator. Those kind of bees are deadly. We wipe out the hives when possible. This one is new. They must have moved in after the hurricane."

"Fine with me." Her thigh chose that moment to remind her of the sting. She rubbed the wound and refused to feel any pity for that hive.

Joe didn't wait for her to get her purse. He grabbed it off the counter and opened. He pulled her car keys out of the bag before she found the breath to protest. With her keys dangling from one hand, he tossed her purse towards her chest with the other.

Amber caught it as he captured her hand and pulled her behind him. The front door was opened before she could dig her heels in to stop the man. Not that she had much of a chance of doing that. Her head didn't even reach his shoulders. His hand closed all the way around hers.

The front door opened and his body surged forward. He pulled her right along behind him. The man had her car unlocked in mere seconds.

"Get in."

He rolled right over the hood of the vehicle before yanking the driver's door open. The rising sound of buzzing made Amber eager to comply. She slammed her door shut as the dark cloud rose over the top of her house. Joe slammed his door so hard the car rocked. The bees swarmed around the car as Joe flipped all the vents closed.

"I agree, call the exterminator." The insects were hostile little buggers. There was nothing sweet or fuzzy about them. Their honey was probably poisonous. The car was surrounded by them as they tried to find a way in.

The ignition turned over as a muffled curse came from Joe. Turning around she giggled at the sight of the man in her car. He was bent over with his knees up around the steering wheel. He scowled at her from his bent position before searching for the gearshift and putting the car in reverse.

"Amber, I'm driving my truck when I take you out for dinner."

"Excuse me, when did I accept a date from you?"

His eyes slipped down her body. Her cheeks flooded with heat in response. His hand suddenly caught her chin in a firm grasp as his mouth captured hers. The kiss was hard and deep. Her body responded immediately to his making her jerk away from him.

Her head bumped into the door making her grumble. Joe smirked at her before he turned his attention back to his driving. "We sort of passed the date stage, but that doesn't mean we can't enjoy a good meal." His dark eyes dropped down to her nipples as his lips thinned. "I think we might need the energy."

The pure confidence displayed by his smug grin made her temper explode. The bees followed the car as they backed down the driveway, trapping her inside with the testosterone ape.

"I bet they don't have killer bees in Idaho."

Chapter Six

"Forget it."

Joe curled his lips back to flash her his teeth instead. His arms were crossed over his chest as he peered at her with those jet-black eyes. His feet were shoulder span apart but he had to look down to see her.

"I mean it, I will go to a motel."

"They're all full for a hundred miles around. I checked. Told you your house wasn't the only house Ruth demolished around here."

Her Little Red temper was simmering. Joe almost laughed out loud. He was getting kind of attached to her extremes in mood. Some of them were downright addictive. Sucking on those sweet coral nipples made her blood boil. His too, when she was nude and begging for more. Even her determination to captain her own ship amused him…right up until it involved her leaving his house.

Amber hated it when he was a step ahead of her too. Her temper tried to find an outlet but she couldn't. The exterminator's team was firebombing the tree in her backyard. Any drones that escaped the extermination were going to be extremely hostile for the next few days until they died naturally.

So, she couldn't go home. The main house was far enough away from the hive that the bees wouldn't bother it. That left her homeless…again.

Idaho was looking better all the time.

"Frank, tell your mama to stop being stubborn."

"My tortoise is named Flamingo!" Her pet! No way was Joe going to name her baby! Who did he think he was anyway? The extermination team had brought her pet over after loading the tortoise onto a dolly. Flamingo was sitting on the hardwood floor of Joe's living room as Amber tried to decide what to do now. Her entire possessions consisted of a giant tortoise and a suitcase.

"Only if he's a homosexual tortoise, and I don't think there is such a thing. Besides, no male should have to be called Flamingo. It's bad enough the guy is making do with a basketball for a woman." Joe aimed a pat at Flamingo but the reptile hissed and pulled his head into his shell. He frowned but bent to pick up her suitcase next. Amber tried to beat him to it but just ended up against him with the case smashed flat against his chest. His eyes lowered to her mouth making her shiver.

Her logical brain was doing a remarkable job of ignoring their afternoon event. Everyone had moments of insanity during life and death crises. It was just that inbred drive for survival and absolutely nothing else.

His black eyes traced her lips with slow detail before slicing into her eyes.

"You leave it up to me and this case is going in my bedroom. Right next to my bed."

"Guestroom sounds great." She pushed away from her bag. There was just no way she was going to win in a game of tug-of-war with him. She would have to outwit the poor male instead.

"Coward."

"Excuse me?"

He turned in the doorjamb and aimed those eyes at her again. He let them slip down her body until they settled over her nipples. His mouth curved slightly until he looked hungry.

"You heard me, Amber. I warned you that I'm not some little boy to twist around your finger. We've got ourselves some business to finish." His eyes sliced back into hers as she felt her nipple rise to stiff attention. "We'll be getting to that as soon as I get things settled, and that is a promise, honey."

* * * * *

Guestroom. Like hell. Joe sat her case in the empty room next to his. His temper itched. A sarcastic grin twisted his lips as he admitted that wasn't the only thing Little Red made itch.

He couldn't wait to get back inside her. At thirty-four he wasn't used to his cock trying to rule his brain. That kind of constant hard-on was for the adolescent crowd.

Well, Little Red was gaining his full attention. He adjusted his fly as he looked around his room. Eight years in the Navy had taught him one thing, all right. Stow your gear and clean your rack. The bedroom was neat, if a little lacking in decorating touches.

Well, Amber had a flare for brightening up a place.

Joe took a deep breath in response to that thought. It had just sort of appeared in his skull. His flannel comforter caught his eye as he envisioned some satin and lace puff-ball on the bed instead.

He shook his head but grinned as he thought about those stunning nude breasts of hers right in the middle of it all. All her creamy skin bare against that satin would make it worth the effort of sleeping in it.

* * * * *

Amber stared at the black smoke rising above her little home. She groaned low and deep but that didn't make her feel much better. She kept staring at that smoke until boredom forced her to abandon the post.

Amber just didn't want to look around the house. It was his house. She felt a tiny quiver of fear in her stomach as she looked around the place. She wasn't even sure what frightened her. The fact that she was there or the idea that Joe might send her on her way when the bees were gone.

It shouldn't matter to her. The event in her kitchen shouldn't matter either. Oh, who was she kidding? The *event* in her kitchen was the highlight of her admittedly limited sexual escapades. She had never even suspected her body could feel like that. If she had, there would have been a whole lot more *events* and escapades in her past.

Her legs were still wobbly. Who would have thought that such an irritating man would be able to turn her knees to liquid? Why couldn't her knees shake for Donald Wilten? Now, there was a friendly guy who had a good sense of humor and a sensitive side. But the guy kissed like a frog and didn't even raise one of her nipples, much less her blood pressure.

Joe raised everything from her temper to the hair on her neck. The man was obnoxious, stubborn and practically a barbarian. She doubted he even understood negotiation in a relationship. He probably had a tattoo that said "My way or the highway".

That wasn't fair. Next thing she knew, she might end up liking him.

"There's wireless internet in my office and the room next to it. Make yourself at home. I'm going to get some work done as well."

Joe watched the way she looked at the front door before looking back at him. He kept his body halfway in the doorframe. She was still too nervous to suit him.

She was staying. The woman didn't have anywhere to go and it bothered the hell out of him that she was even considering turning down his offer. A week ago he never would have considered sharing his home with any female. Little Red was different.

"Might as well settle down, honey, we're going to be keeping company for a while."

"I could just move to Idaho."

A small smile appeared on his face. The expression sent a chill down her spine. There was an aggressive male staring out of his eyes right now. One who considered her his prey. "Amber, my darling. I am beginning to get the idea that you just enjoy conflict." Joe stepped closer and a smack landed on her bottom. Amber jumped back as Joe kept smiling at her.

Her body responded bluntly to the knowledge of his pursuit. Her breasts slowly began swelling, making themselves more noticeable for his eyes. The walls of her passage felt empty again as she felt the smooth slide of fluid easing over the sensitive skin. Reminding her of the sheer bliss of his possession.

"You have to stay until you testify."

That was true enough. The court system had plenty of rights for criminals but not a whole lot for witnesses. She was tethered to the case with a chain of legal mumbo jumbo that all translated out into the fact that she was stuck.

"Yeah, I know it."

He chuckled at her. Those long legs closed the distance between them before his warm hand cupped her chin. His eyes cut into hers as she surrendered to the urge to stick her lower lip out.

"Where's my Little Red's spirit?"

"Auburn!"

His mouth caught hers as he pulled her body into his embrace. His lips took a slow, lingering kiss from her as she wiggled against the rising heat.

"It's red, everywhere." His lips nipped her neck before lifting to her face again. "There's baby-soft red hair on the top of your arms. I bet it grows on those amazing legs of yours too but you shave it away, and honey, those little red curls sitting between your thighs are the sweetest things I've ever seen."

"I am going to wax!"

He threw his head back and laughed at her announcement. A second later she gasped as a hand cupped her bottom and pressed her along his length. The hard erection hidden in his jeans pressed into her belly. His eyes glittered as he watched her face reflect that knowledge.

"That could be a whole lot of fun, too. Go right ahead and lose those little curls. It would be sexy as all hell." Another smack hit her bottom making her gasp. "See what I mean? You just enjoy rocking the boat. Don't matter what I say."

A phone rang, making him cuss softly. His fingers gently gripped her bottom before he spun her loose.

"That's my office line." Joe's face suddenly transformed as he looked at her. "I want you to let me know if you step outside."

"I don't need your permission." She announced her words to an empty room. She didn't need his approval to go where she wanted to go or to change her body! Her cheeks stung as a vivid picture emerged in her imagination. Just what exactly would he do if she waxed? More importantly, what wouldn't he do?

* * * * *

"Josiah, my boy, you make me a happy governor."

"Thank you, sir."

A loud boom of amusement rolled out of his uncle's chest. "I want to know how you caught that damn weasel. I told you he was using Pullman for the transfers, didn't I? Damn it, I'm going to make it stick this time!"

Through a rather odd turn of events, Timothy Lott had ended up in the governor's chair. The man's true love was law enforcement and it shone in his words over the phone line. The man held a personal vendetta for the drug traders who used Texas to smuggle their goods into the nation via Mexico.

"Dantrolp is going to do some time and you, my boy, have earned your office."

"Now hold on a second." Joe knew where his uncle was heading with that comment.

"Now just listen up, Josiah. You're out of the service now and need to think about settling down. How's that girl you met? Your mother says the rumor is she's a pretty little thing."

Joe squeezed the bridge of his nose and resisted the urge to deny any interest in Amber. The afternoon in her kitchen would make a liar out of him immediately. But he wasn't in the mood to share his interest in her with anyone right at the moment. What was going one between them was theirs to deal with. The rest of the world needed to take a hike.

"Tell my mom to hold off on ordering those wedding invitations. I just met her a week ago."

His uncle laughed in a low male tone. Joe heard the springs on the man's chair groan as he leaned back in it. "Joe, cut the crap. A week is all it takes but you can get around to telling me to mind my own business."

"Glad to hear it."

His uncle laughed again. "Where is the witness staying?"

"Well, as it turns out, my place." Joe didn't bother to sound sorry about that fact. "Got a beehive on the back property, so I moved her into the main house while it's being exterminated."

"Same gal? Well, now that ought to make things more interesting. But I like the sound of it. Dantrolp is connected to half the scum in the underworld. I like the idea of her under your eye a whole lot." The desk chair groaned again. "Got to run, these people keep me on so short a leash, it makes a rubber band look long."

The line went dead making Joe shake his head. Family was the worst. You couldn't tell them to get lost. Even if you did, they didn't have to listen because they were kin. Sticking their fingers in your life wasn't just normal, it was expected.

He still wasn't sure about being Sheriff. There had been no one interested in running for the position — there still wasn't.

Maybe his uncle had a point. It was time to think about setting his own roots down. Looking around the ranch-style home, Joe considered how quiet it was. It was the house his uncle had raised his kids in. That's what made the Governor take Pullman County so personally. Quiet and remote, it was a simple place that lacked the complex problems of the urban bustle.

Yeah, maybe it was time to do some thinking about that. There was a soft brush and thump on the other side of the wall. The corners of his mouth rose as he listened to the soft evidence that Amber was setting up her laptop computer.

He liked the idea far too much. Enjoyment rushed through his veins like fine tequila, warm and heating his skin. It was like he could smell the delicate scent of her. Drifting through the house, it made his cock tighten with the certain knowledge that he'd get the chance to taste her again.

His uncle's words made him grin. Any reason to tighten his rope on Little Red was good but his gut twisted just the slightest amount as he considered Dantrolp. The man did have a history of making witnesses disappear.

Reaching for the phone, Joe punched in a number. Privacy just might need to wait until he was sure Dantrolp didn't have any devoted friends out there.

There was a scratch and thump on the floorboards as Flamingo poked his head into the office. Joe punched in another line of numbers when his call connected and hung up. The tortoise ambled into the office, sniffing as it went.

"So, what's your price, Frank?" The tortoise didn't retract into its shell this time. Joe reached for its head and scratched it like Amber did. The tortoise sniffed his fingers before giving a short hiss. "I see, let's see what I've got in the kitchen."

Standing up, Joe moved towards the door but stopped as his ears detected the movements of the tortoise. Looking back, he watched the large reptile turn his shell around and begin to follow.

"I could get used to you, Frank."

* * * * *

"You must be Amber."

Only a mother could sound that cheerful. Amber turned and looked into the eyes of a woman who had the same dark eyes as Joe. She just walked into the house with a ring of keys dangling from her fingers as she hugged a large paper bag in her hands.

"I'm Deborah, Josiah's mother." She certainly must be. The woman walked right on into the kitchen. She halted in the hallway and called out to her son.

"Josiah! It's your mother! Don't shoot me."

She turned and winked. "Of course he probably saw my car pull up. It's near impossible to sneak up on that son of mine now. Whatever it is they teach those boys in SEAL training, it certainly cures them of the need to be reminded to pay attention!" She smiled before taking her bag towards the kitchen.

"Come along, dear, I brought you Josiah's favorite chicken dish for supper and I even wrote the recipe down for you."

Deborah walked through the double doorway that led to the kitchen. Amber started to follow when she caught Joe standing in the hallway. The frozen look of horror on his face made her giggle. She stuffed her fist against her lips as he tried to think of some way to prevent her from going to talk to his mother.

"Be right there, Mrs. Lott." Joe frowned at her as he began walking towards her. Amber offered him a bright smile before jumping out of his reach.

"I sure hope she brought some of your baby pictures." Amber whispered her words and listened to Joe smother his cussing. "Naked ones."

"If you want to see skin, honey, just ask."

That little grin was back on his lips. The expression had been around since the *event* in her kitchen. The current topic certainly wasn't one she was having while his mother was in the next room. In fact, they weren't having it at all, ever.

Amber stepped towards the kitchen and the clink of dishes. Anyone who volunteered to cook dinner was her immediate friend. If they also managed to outmaneuver Sheriff Joe, they were on their way to being her best friend. But her temper flared as Joe made a few clucking sounds in response to her retreat. She flung him a heated look but he simply raised a dark eyebrow at her anger.

Deborah smiled at her and Amber felt her blood chill. Her eyes made a brief inspection of her body before that smile brightened. The woman was hunting for a daughter-in-law, all right.

"Josiah is my oldest boy and I'm so proud of his manners. Did he tell you that this was my father's house?"

"No." Amber stepped forward as the woman waved her towards the dinner preparation.

"Yes, I grew up here with three pigheaded brothers, but I forgive them because I know now that I was born and they were hatched."

Amber giggled. She couldn't help it. Deborah had a wicked sense of humor.

"It's good to see the house used. When my brother became Governor, it ended up vacant. A home should never be empty."

That made her chest tighten. Amber already liked the house. It wasn't because of the modern edges, but she loved the wood floors that covered it. That older shade of hardwood that spoke of years of use with its small little scars. Joe must have painted the walls because they were creamy beige and spotless. There were also large ceiling fans in every room, the kind with wicker blades attached to them.

"Now, I've brought everything for dinner. Josiah loves to eat. You'll want to keep this recipe card handy. I'll email you a few more but I'm sure you have your own family recipes to try out on him."

"Hmm, not really. I don't cook much."

"Well, my dear, we are going to have to change that! Josiah is part grizzly bear—feed him or he growls."

Amber thought about setting the woman straight. She really did. There was just something about Deborah that told her she'd be wasting her time. The woman had decided to play matchmaker and nothing Amber said was going to break through her plans.

On the upside, there was dinner involved. On the downside, she wasn't exactly in the mood to deal with a kitchen counter just yet, and certainly not in front of Joe's mother.

A soft footfall behind her made her face flush. Deborah was rattling off the cooking instructions as she assembled the casserole in a white baking dish. Amber kept her eyes on the process as she tried not to turn around to look at Joe.

She wanted to. There was something...secure about keeping an eye on him. Maybe it was some idea that she might be able to maintain her sanity if she kept out of his reach. For some reason, his touch caused her brain to fall into a coma. All she seemed to do was react on some primitive level that she'd only discovered she had since meeting Joe. But his mother's word floated across her memory as she peeked sideways at him. SEAL? You heard about Navy SEALs in movies and read about them in books but girls didn't run into them just by chance. At least, Amber didn't think that sort of trained man carried tortoises up hills very often.

It fit him though. Amber looked at the hard body and the way Joe moved his eyes. Yeah, SEAL fit. It wasn't that she knew all that much about Navy SEALs, it was just the idea that she got in the pit of her stomach. Joe could be deadly if he needed to be. She saw it in his eyes.

"What on earth is that?"

Joe laughed in the deep amused tone. Amber turned to see his shoulders shaking with his reaction to his mother's first sight of Flamingo. Her pet had wandered into the kitchen, drawn by the conversation.

"That's Frank, Amber's pet."

"Shouldn't that animal be in a zoo?"

Joe reached down and scratched the tortoise's head. Flamingo stretched his neck out for the attention. Amber glared at her pet. Joe smirked back at her as he continued to rub along Flamingo's head.

"Nope, Frank is a yard tortoise. Kind of like a dog, only vegetarian with a shell." Joe winked at Amber. "And he really likes cantaloupe."

Oh, unfair! Amber glared at her pet but the reptile just moved his head to offer the other side to Joe. Flamingo would roll over for anyone that brought him cantaloupe.

"I see." Deborah lifted her masterpiece and placed it into the oven. She turned and looked at the tortoise again. "I do believe he must outweigh you, my dear."

Deborah suddenly smiled that bright smile again before she reached up to hug her son. Joe had to lean over for the embrace. She was heading for the front door a second later. Amber felt her blood surge forward as she understood that the woman fully intended to leave her and Joe alone.

The reason for the privacy was pathetically obvious in the woman's gleeful expression. Her cell phone chimed for attention and she eagerly ran down the hallway to answer it before her voice mail caught the call.

Joe watched her run. His skin tightened as he pressed his boots into the floorboards. He wanted to chase her. That idea made him snarl. He hardly recognized it as his own and it was pure reaction. He enjoyed the burn of need as he listened to her voice on the phone. Yeah, he'd like to chase her down the hallway and right into the bedroom.

His cock began to stiffen as he considered her sleeping under his roof. That knowledge was practically mind-numbing. It seeped into his brain and turned off every gentle maneuver he knew to court a woman. Instead he wanted to hunt her. Use every skill he'd ever learned in the Navy to stalk her and corner his prey before she even knew what kind of predator was scenting her.

A grimace twisted his mouth as he gave the fly of his jeans a pull. He'd get the chance, maybe not tonight, but her little hard nipples told him it wasn't a one-sided desire.

Joe just needed to stay sane long enough to see her accept what her body already knew.

Life could be a real bitch at times.

* * * * *

She managed to ignore Joe for five whole hours. The man was giving her less and less space to do it in as the night went on. An odd pulse of electricity shot down her spine as she noticed his slowly decreasing circling. It was almost excitement but Amber refused to label it such.

Her behavior left a lot to be desired. Amber checked her email account for the thirtieth time before letting out a sigh. She was inventing things to do in order to ignore the man sharing the house with her. That didn't make any sense. She was an adult and well past the age when sex was considered immoral.

It was just so intense with Joe. Sex became some kind of mind-shattering experience that left her clinging to him. The way her body responded to him gave him so much power over her. That scared her right down to her toes.

Wanting to have a relationship with the man that included sex was one thing. Needing that man and craving him was another.

It was dark and quiet tonight. There was almost no moon in the sky. Only the hint of a breeze blew in the open window next to her desk. An odd scrape and shuffle came to her ears as some kind of muffled noise.

Amber looked at the window and pushed her chair back. Her fingers were just moving the sheer curtain aside when she was pulled away from the window and back into the hallway.

"Don't move."

Her back was flat against the wall with one hard hand over her chest. Light spilled out of her room and onto Joe's face. There wasn't a hint of the man she knew. His opposite hand held a gun as his head angled to catch any further sounds coming through the window.

His eyes were hard as stone and his face expressionless. Every muscle in his body was tight and ready to spring. Whatever strength she'd guessed he might have in all those muscles it was clearly displayed at that moment.

It sent a shiver down her spine. This man was deadly. Another sound hit their ears and Joe reacted to it. His eyes caught hers as he turned towards the sound again.

His hand pulled the hall coat closet open but his eyes were still moving over the hallway and doorways with razor-sharp movements. "In and don't move."

He didn't wait for her to comply. Instead one solid hand grasped her arm and pushed her into the closet. There were only a few things hanging in it. Joe kept pushing her until her back hit the wall. He released her and pulled the clothing in front of her. "I mean it, Amber. Don't even think about coming out. Someone is on the property. Backup will be here soon."

The door shut and with it went any scrap of light. Hiding in a closet made her temper rise but she clamped her common sense down onto it. The sight of that pistol in Joe's hand was all she needed to resign herself to staying exactly where he'd put her.

Seconds moved by like hours. Each and every noise was horribly loud. She was certain her own breathing could be heard as far away as the kitchen. Amber shook her head and tried to think of anything but the hunt going on in the darkened yard. She held no doubt that Joe was stalking his intruders. All of the tight muscles that turned her knees to jelly suddenly hit her as the weapons of a trained warrior. The word SEAL was more than a title — most importantly, an honor that Joe had earned.

* * * * *

There were things a man never left behind him. Joe hit a knee with one eye on the sight of his pistol. He scanned the yard and waited. A crunch of gravel sent him at a dead run for the opposite side of the yard. The fence came into sight and he watched a boot disappear over its top.

One well-placed step and Joe was head high with the top of the barrier, pistol muzzle first. Tires squealed as an old truck punched its accelerator with one man still scrambling to get into the passenger side. He pulled his legs in as the truck took the corner on two wheels. Joe squeezed off two rounds but missed the back tire. Damn truck was fishtailing too much for a clean shot.

Yanking his radio off his hip he depressed the transmit button.

"Suspect is northbound. Twin-cab truck, no back license plate."

"Ten-four."

A sharp sting hit his arm making him snarl. The damn bees were returning after foraging and finding their hive destroyed. Jumping down, Joe sprinted back across the yard until he was far enough away from the kamikaze insects. He listened to his deputies as they tried to pick up his suspect vehicle.

He cussed as it looked like luck wasn't his friend tonight. Using a flashlight, he inspected the ground between the main house and his guesthouse. There wasn't a single sign of any fresh movement.

Whoever they were, they'd come over the back fence and discovered the unhappy bees. At the moment, Joe was kind of fond of the little devils. Amber wasn't in the guesthouse due to their presence and for that he owed them a pleasant thought.

Turning on his heel, he headed back towards the object of his thoughts. It could have been a random burglary but that would be too much of a coincidence.

Dantrolp had the reputation of never getting convicted, and unless Joe missed his guess, the man was trying to ensure his record stayed clean.

Amber blinked as Joe opened the door. Joe let his temper erupt into rage at the sight of her nervous face. Those blue eyes flickered over the space behind him before she let him pull her out of her hiding place.

He wanted to kill in that moment. Whatever the reason, he didn't like his woman being scared and certainly not under his roof. He wasn't exactly sure when he'd begun thinking of Amber in the terms of his, but he was and that was all he cared about right now. He would have taken any threat to one of his citizens as important. The fact that it happened to be Amber made it personal.

"Did you catch them?" Amber still wasn't exactly sure there had been someone to capture but the serious look on Joe's face made her nervous. The man looked dangerous, and in an odd way she almost felt his presence. Her skin tightened in some kind of primitive response to the raw power his body was radiating.

"No." His hand caught the back of her neck in a smooth stroke that made her shiver. He repeated the motion before grasping her arm again and leading her towards the kitchen. The light was on, making her blink as her eyes tried to adjust to the brightness.

The hand on her arm was firm. Everything about Joe seemed too precise, too rigid, but she wasn't in the mood to cross him. Instinct told her she'd lose the battle.

The way he kept watching everything around them was too polished to be argued with. He had a systematic movement of eyes and body that formed an almost perfect system of observation. He was relaxed yet poised on the edge of springing into action. He definitely suited the badge she'd seen on his wide chest that first moment out on that highway. Somehow, she'd pushed that image aside.

Tonight it was radiating over her face. Maybe she didn't want to see him as such a hardened male. Men like this were the kind that women adjusted to and negotiation was completely nonexistent.

Another shiver shook her spine and his eyes instantly caught the tiny telltale motion of weakness. His dark eyes rested on her, taking in details. Her breasts gently swelled under their weight as her nipples tightened in response to his raw strength. Her body was frantic to attract his attention and somewhere in her brain she recognized that she did like him. She trusted this man and it was a deep emotion that was growing every time he didn't let her twist him with her demands.

Joe's senses were tight and ultra-keen. Years of application had sharpened them until his body knew exactly how to respond in moments of danger. Joe indulged the hard bite of arousal that always followed being on the edge. That was part of the survival instinct. When you went into battle, your life hung in the balance. When you came away alive, your cock wanted to reap the rewards of coming out on top.

The hard points of Amber's nipples burned into his brain as he rode the wave of tight arousal. It was almost overwhelming as he watched her little tongue appear to run over her bottom lip. The way she used that soft tongue rose in his memory while he tried to hold off the image. His men would be knocking on the door any second and Joe needed to keep at least half his mind off Amber's coral nipples.

For the moment anyway. A little while later he'd be happy to confront that flicker of defiance still sparkling in her eyes. In fact, his cock twitched with the idea of applying another hard kiss to her lips as she tried to find enough willpower to ignore the desire twisting her little coral nipples.

A fist landed on the back door. Amber jumped in response. The tension between her and Joe had tightened to such a degree, she'd simply forgotten the fact that he said he'd called backup. Her body sent out a whimper at the arrival of company. Amber pushed her lips into a pout at the very real disappointment racing along her skin. She needed to move to Idaho really soon.

Before she fell in love with him.

Grasping at her resolution, Amber headed for the kitchen door and away from the men filtering into it. She tried to ignore the lament her emotions raised over leaving Joe. She couldn't go falling in love. That kind of thing only ended a girl up in trouble. Besides, with the set of shoulders Joe had, a sassy-mouthed girl wouldn't be the one to get a ring out of the man. A solid grip caught her arm.

"Where are you going?"

Joe's voice was whisper-soft but it grated on her nerves. She glared at the hand holding her in place.

"Excuse me, I didn't know I needed permission to leave your sight, Sheriff."

Joe's eyes darkened with hard promise as he stepped closer to her. "At the moment you do."

A shiver tried to shake her and Amber stomped her foot with displeasure. This was ridiculous! She couldn't decide if she wanted to scream at him or claw at the shirt covering his chest. Her body was twisting as a current of energy pulsed through it. Standing still was impossible.

"I haven't got much worth stealing, besides, they'll just go find some place without bees to rob."

Joe didn't say anything. Instead his eyes turned hard as they looked at her. The expression in those black depths scared her more than any words might have.

"I was going to take a shower."

Joe gave her a sharp nod of his head as his fingers released her arm. She shouldn't have needed to tell him where she was going. Her temper didn't rise up in defense of her pride, instead all she found lingering in her head was the idea that she didn't want to have any kind of confrontation in front of his men. Just when she'd developed concern for his image, she didn't know. Maybe it didn't matter.

Joe watched that perfect bottom disappear before clamping his control firmly in place. He was going to be finding plenty of opportunity to be close to that sassy little backside. Dantrolp had just given him every reason to stick to Little Red like a puppy. His gut was telling him the evening entertainment had been carefully planned to end any further threat to the scum's freedom.

The shower turned on as Joe turned towards his men and the need to collect some kind of evidence. His opinion wasn't enough to place Amber under his protection even if he wanted it to be. Little Red would delight in casting her own view of the break-in. It was his job to point out her mistakes.

It was going to be his pleasure.

Chapter Seven

"Do you know how to use a gun?"

Amber jumped and glared at him. Joe didn't seem to care that she was miffed with his sudden appearance. Instead she caught a flicker of pride in his eyes. He moved past the doorway of her room, making her nervous. She tightened the grip on her towel as the room shrunk now that he was in it. Her skin became ultra-aware of how little effort it would take to lose her towel. She shifted as the folds of her sex began to heat and feel too swollen with her thighs pressed together.

"No. I don't like weapons."

"How do you know you don't like them?"

"Well, I just decided I don't like them." Joe gave her a harassed look. She tossed her head in response. Amber didn't like the little twist of fear that was currently trying to take root in her brain.

"Fine, have it your way."

"What does that mean?"

His lips rose at the corners as he took another step closer. Her nipples drew taut beneath the terrycloth of her towel, making her cheeks flood with color. She was noticing how strong and wide his chest was again. Her nose even detected the clean scent of his warm male skin. It traveled down from her senses to her belly where it erupted into heat inside her passage. Fluid coated the walls making her feel incredibly empty. Naughty little whispers bounced off the corners of her brain as the event in her kitchen inspired the desire for more escapades.

"What's the problem, Amber? Aren't you happy that I agree with you?"

His voice dipped as he stepped one pace closer to her again. Her feet itched to move but her body begged her to stand still. It was a tangle of conflicting needs that raced from her brain through her body. One set of emotions aimed at fleeing from his much stronger body and the other set intent on sampling that strength in the most primitive of manners. Her disobedient eyes actually dropped to the front of his jeans. The fabric bulged out making her passage ache for the swollen flesh.

Joe caught her chin and raised her face to his. His eyes were twin flames of heat that drilled into hers as he stepped forward until they were almost touching.

"I could show you how to handle a pistol, honey, but I think I might enjoy sticking close to you instead."

"Those lessons you mentioned…when are we starting?"

Joe cocked his head to the side and pulled his gun from where it was tucked into the waistband of his jeans. Amber reached for the weapon but Joe didn't give it to her. Instead he placed the gun in her hands and cupped his hands over hers. His fingers firmly pressed on her hands until she gripped the pistol correctly. His lean body moved behind hers as he slipped those hands over her frame, adjusting her stance and position to his liking.

"Line up the sights." His voice brushed past her ear as he leaned over her shoulder to see if she was looking down the barrel of the gun.

The fingers that corrected her position weren't the impersonal ones of a trainer. Joe smoothed each touch over her skin just like he had that afternoon. Her skin rose into delighted little bumps as pleasure zipped along her nerves from each touch. His hips brushed hers making her body tremble with just a hint of hard male erection against her bottom. Her body jumped with need as one cheek of her bottom delighted in transmitting the feel of his cock to the rest of her body.

"Don't lose your focus, baby. Steady with the grip, line up the sights."

Amber gritted her teeth as she tried to ignore the ripple of pleasure his breath sent across her bare neck. Her nipples drew into little buttons as they clamored for his hands to correct them as well. Her hips gave an instinctive little wiggle as Joe brushed against her bottom once again. Amber couldn't stop the telltale motion, her body refused to resist rubbing across the hard length of his erection.

Joe laughed in a deep husky tone as his entire back came into contact with her body. His hands covered hers again as the brush of his breath hit her temple. His hips bumped against hers as she almost purred with the delight of so much contact. That hard cock was pressed to both sides of her bottom making her sweat as the towel became almost unbearable to keep on.

"That's it, honey, but I have a little confession to make. I'd rather just get naked with you."

Oh yes!!!

Amber bit her tongue and struggled to keep her body under some kind of rational control. Her self-restraint had eroded as the ripples of pleasure coursed through her body and joined into a river that flowed between her breasts and her passage. The hard cock throbbing against her bottom tempted and promised more delight, if she would just forget about control.

"We are not getting…undressed!"

Joe laughed at her words and shifted as he tucked his gun into the back of his waistband and pulled her closer. One arm snaked around her waist to hold her in place as he let go of her chin and stroked his warm fingers down her throat. His fingers touched her chest and kept going until they found a hard little nipple beneath her towel. His thumb gently circled the nub, making her squirm against the sudden, almost painful need that simple touch produced. Fluid actually began seeping down the walls of her passage like honey. She felt it on the top of her thighs as a tremor shook her body.

"This little nipple thinks we should get naked." The hard cock in his pants agreed. Joe pressed her along his length as he caught her denial with his mouth. Her lips parted as he captured the back of her head and held her in place for his kiss. He growled against the soft lips that opened to admit the thrust of his tongue. Need was raging against the chain he'd used to hold it. Had it really only been that afternoon that he'd had her? It seemed far too long since he'd listened to the little whimpers of pleasure that were beginning to emerge from her throat.

Joe rubbed a thumb over one nipple and watched Amber gasp. Her swollen lips formed a little round expression as he pushed the terrycloth away from the coral tip. "I love the way your nipples get hard for me, baby." His eyes turned hard as his thumb rubbed across the bare tip. "These little buttons drive me insane with the need to get inside you."

Amber blinked as she tried to remember just why she needed to keep her stupid towel. It was wet and clammy against her skin. Her hands had left the top of it to spread along the wide shoulders that beckoned for her touch.

One tug and Joe sent the towel towards the floor. He bent and swung her bare body up against his before angling her through the doorway. The sight of his bed snapped her back into reality. It was like crossing the doorway leading to the master bedroom was a form of declaration. Almost like an act of submission.

"Just hold on. Red light!"

Joe tossed her onto his bed in response. Amber bounced in a tangle of limbs before tossing her hair out of her face. The look on his face made her wish she'd left the auburn curtain in front of her eyes.

"Red light? What the devil is that supposed to mean?"

Beyond torture. She was stunning, completely bare and in his bed. Instinct bubbled over his control with the need to take. The little red curls at the apex of her thighs beckoned to him as her breasts thrust their coral nipples towards him. Joe didn't give a damn what her mouth said. He could smell how wet she was.

"What do you think it means?"

That wasn't the right thing to say. His eyes actually glowed as he thought about what he wanted her to mean. She swallowed roughly as his eyes stroked her body, lingering over her breasts. Memory surfaced with acute recollection of the feel of his firm lips on her nipples. Heat poured towards her belly as his eyes traveled down her until they reached the barrier of her closed thighs.

Her reaction to him was written on her face. Joe felt his lips curl back from his teeth as he watched the blush spread down from her face until it turned the creamy mounds of her breasts pink.

"I think it means, talking is a waste of time, honey." It was also driving him insane. He could smell her body, the heat that proclaimed the interest her words were attempting to deny. His shirt scratched against skin that was too hot for any kind of civilized modesty. Joe ripped the garment open. Her eyes dropped to his chest as that little pink tongue appeared to moisten her lower lip. "I think it means you need a little work on expressing your emotions, honey. Your mouth says back off and your nipples say…suck me."

She gasped again, this time her face turned as red as her hair as Joe moved his hand to his belt buckle and opened it.

"Were you sure about that color?" Joe popped one single button of his fly open and her eyes flew to the small gap he'd opened. "Maybe we should try yellow. I could spend at least an hour on yellow." Two more buttons popped as she licked her upper lip. "There're a whole lot of places on that lovely body that I could spend my time lingering over while we wait for that light to turn green. No hurry at all."

Fear ignited as she looked at his face. The skin was drawn tight as he considered just exactly how to make good on his words. There wasn't a single doubt in her mind that this man could do exactly as he said. The need to refuse bubbled up in her throat.

"I'd like to see you try."

She wasn't sure just why she wanted to throw another gauntlet down at his feet. There was a demon inside her, urging her to question this man's abilities to master her flesh.

Joe popped the last button free in response. Her skin tightened almost unbearably as she waited for his jeans to release his swollen cock. Instead the fabric held and teased her with its straining edges.

"So would I." His words were harsh. That tingle of fear brightened as he shucked his jeans and his entire body came into view. He was so completely male. Amber actually felt her nipples tighten for him. Deep inside her most secret passage an ache clamored for the attention of the male in front of her. This wasn't about civilized conversation or choices. Everything she thought she wanted in a lover condensed down to the sheer need her body felt for Joe. She wanted his weight pressing her down as his hips spread her thighs for that cock.

His hands were hot. So strong yet controlled as he handled her. Joe captured her shoulders as the bed gave under his weight. A tiny moan escaped through her lips before he caught her mouth and claimed it with his. His tongue stabbed deeply into her mouth as he caught his weight on his bent elbows. The wide expanse of his chest hovered above her while the crisp hair covering it teased her ultrasensitive breasts.

He wanted to taste her. Joe lingered over her mouth, teasing the surface of her lips as he coaxed her to open them completely. Right here, words didn't matter. He thrust his tongue deeply into her mouth as he indulged himself in the pure sensation of male to female. Her thighs rose on either side of his hips as she cradled his body against the hot opening that begged for possession. His fingers twisted in her hair as he held her in place while he continued the kiss. It fed his need. She surrounded him with her taste while the scent of her open body rose between her spread thighs. His cock swelled tighter as he trailed his mouth over the column of her throat. He enjoyed the bite of arousal. Joe wanted to let it twist and burn while he took her to the edge of reason.

"Do you have any idea how sweet your nipples are?" Joe nuzzled the mound of a breast as Amber found her hands twisting over his shoulders. Her back arched without conscious thought, offering the aching nub to his mouth. He didn't end her torment of longing, instead his fingers tightened in her hair as his eyes captured her.

"Those little nipples are hard enough to cut glass with. I could spend a long time just licking them." He meant it too. Regret for her hasty words wasn't enough to conquer the flame of excitement that raced along her spine. He watched it burn in her eyes before dropping his lips to one coral tip. His warm breath teased it as her back arched almost painfully towards the promise of pleasure from those firm lips. "After that, I'd enjoy sucking them."

Instead the tip of his tongue gently touched the top of one beaded nipple. He drew the rough surface over the top of her before licking around the little nub. A moan rose clear and long from her throat and his chest shook with amusement. His hands slipped from her hair and under her back as he held her up for his attention.

His lips still didn't close around his chosen treat. He licked its top and around its swollen center before tasting the puckered edges of her nipple. She hung on sensation so sharp it merged into pain as he moved to her opposite breast.

"That light still yellow?"

She purred at him. Joe gave her nipple another lap before surrendering to the need to wrap his lips over it. His cock gave a jerk as he sucked on her sweet flesh and listened to her whimper. Maybe it was supposed to be a battle. Consensual sex had never felt so hot. Right then he wanted to make her yield. Take back the restraining words that she'd hurled at his feet while her hard nipples thrust up in invitation.

The hot scent of arousal filled his head and he followed it down her body. Joe lifted her hips as he licked and tasted the satin covering her belly. The crisp curls covering her mons smelled so damn sexy.

There was a naughty delight spreading through her as Amber held back the words he was waiting for. She wanted him so bad but needed to play with his control just as much.

"It's green!" She couldn't take what his warm breath promised her he intended. His breath hit the spread opening of her body and she twisted as sensation shot straight into her core. She balanced on the edge of insanity as her imagination delighted in conjuring up what he might do with his tongue between her thighs.

"Glad to hear it."

He growled his words before lifting her hips to his mouth. His dark eyes looked up her body as his breath hit her exposed clit. "I like playing games with you, honey. I like it a whole lot." His eyes lowered to her open sex as Amber felt her breath lodge in her throat. "And I love to win."

She bucked as he caught the first taste of her. Joe tightened his hands and held her for his touch. He found the little nub at the top of her sex and gently sucked it between firm lips. The cry she let out only fueled his determination to taste her pleasure.

"Joe...I can't take it!" The sensation twisted and pulled so tight, she was powerless to control it. Her body seemed to belong only to his will. She had ceased to fear that level of submission. The pleasure coursed over her will as her body tightened further and climax began to bear down on her. Nothing mattered but the shimmering promise of fulfillment.

"Don't worry, baby, I'll hold you while you take it."

His words were as hard as his will. His eyes glittered with promise and triumph as he looked up her body. A second later he dipped his mouth and captured her little pearl between impossibly hot lips. The tip of his tongue joined in the stimulus as she listened to a husky moan rise out of her chest. Her hips thrust towards his mouth as her breath caught in her throat. He released her clit as his tongue made a long lap down her slit to the opening of her passage. He licked it in a slow circle before gently lapping her slit back to the button at the top. "God, you taste good." His hands tightened on her hips as his lips sucked the little nub hard. Amber shattered in a moment of pure sensation, certain that even her heart stopped beating while everything twisted and burned with pleasure.

Her cry pushed his control over the limit. Joe rose above her body and thrust deeply into her. The walls of her passage clung to his cock as he growled with primitive glory. Her thighs gripped his hips as he firmly thrust and rocked inside her. The need to climax burned deep inside him as he listened to the sound of her whimpers.

"I'm really enjoying this yellow light." Amber felt her eyes fly open with horror. He thrust deeply into her body and pulled out on a long, slow stroke. There wasn't even a hint of hurry as she bucked beneath him and twisted in the flame of need. Reaching between their bodies, Joe made sure the lips of her sex were spread open so that each thrust drew across her clit. A whimper rose from her throat as he made sure his thrust remained slow and hard.

"That light turned green, Joe."

"Yeah? I guess I missed that part." His hips flexed as his cock lodged deeply inside her once again. "Doesn't matter, I'm enjoying the ride."

She growled at him. Joe thrust hard into her body as her lips parted in tiny pants. Yeah, he was enjoying every thrust into her wet body and each shudder that shook her as his cock impaled her. But the need to burst inside her made his cock demand he give her what she craved. Leaning over, Joe sucked one coral-tipped breast in his mouth as he thrust hard into her body. He growled around the little tip as Amber whimpered. "All right, baby, I'll take you home now."

He filled her so completely, Amber could only cling to his larger frame as he drove into her with quick thrusts. Her hips lifted for him and told her pride to go to hell. It felt so right to be filled by him, moving with him. The pleasure was deeper this time, more intense and rooted in the very center of her body. She needed it so desperately and he joined her in that quest. His shoulders shook as they both struggled in the last moment of sanity before sensation ruled and they dissolved into the swirling mixture of need and fulfillment. It washed away the barriers between them as they merged into one entity, grasping each other as the ultimate joy enwrapped them both. The hot splash of his seed inside her made her purr with some deeper emotion that had never really shown up before. Amber felt her thighs grasp Joe's hips frantically as he growled and his cock jerked inside her.

Joe rolled off her and pulled her body along with his. Amber squirmed but his hands smoothed her into place next to his warm body. Two little tears stung her eyes as he refused to let her wiggle away. Instead Joe caught the back of her hair and gently pulled until her face lifted to lock eyes with him.

"You have an appointment somewhere?" His eyes were hard as they studied hers.

"I don't need a reason to get up."

He grunted and captured her lips with his. It was a slow and warm kiss that made her skin begin to heat once again. His hand held her head in place as his lips pushed hers apart. He rolled half over her as the fingers in her hair tipped her head up for his mouth.

Joe lifted his head and reached beyond her. The comforter suddenly wrapped over her as he rolled back onto his back. Because they were lying on the bedding, Joe was able to pull the edge of the comforter until she was trapped against his body by it. The solid arm around her waist was strong enough that the fabric trapped her into a cocoon. One of his knees rose between her legs as he kept tugging on that blanket until she was completely bound to his length.

"Then don't go looking for one, honey. We can butt heads tomorrow."

"I think I should sleep in the other room..." The arm around her waist gave a squeeze as his opposite hand caught the back of her head and pushed it down onto a shoulder.

Her words were soft. Joe tipped her chin up to look at her eyes. "Honey, I don't want to know what guy ever made love to you and then let you go sleep in a cold bed. Because I might have to find him and beat the hell out of him." His eyes went hard for a moment before Joe smoothed her closer to his body. A little purr came from her throat as Amber enjoyed the secure clasp of his arm around her shoulders. Joe watched her face before grinning at her and pushing her head back onto his chest. "Get some sleep, honey. I want a rematch of traffic lights later."

She giggled before slipping her fingers through the hair on his chest. That secure feeling coated her thoughts as she felt his hand settle on the curve of her hip. Yeah, she could fall in love with Joe and at that very moment, it felt like a really good idea.

Idaho where?

"Go to sleep, baby."

Joe listened to the sound of her respiration as it grew deeper and lengthened. He looked at the red curls covering his hands and grunted. Her thighs slipped along his, making his cock twitch with renewed hunger. He stroked her head instead and watched the way her eyelashes rested on her cheeks.

She looked so peaceful right then, almost docile. His chest rumbled with amusement. Little Red didn't have a docile fiber in her body! Tomorrow morning she would be as ruffled as a badger with wet fur.

And God help him…he was looking forward to it.

* * * * *

"I am moving to Idaho!" No one heard her. Amber kicked at the bedding and hissed as it held. She was wrapped in the comforter tighter than a newborn. She couldn't even decide how Joe had done it. But all the ends were tucked and folded using her body weight as the force holding her in the center of it. The shower was running in the master bathroom making it the best time to escape without having to face her rash behavior of last night.

She kicked and rolled over. Her cocoon lost some of its strength so she kicked harder and rolled again. She fell off the end of the bed and landed on her knees. A yelp came out of her mouth as the shower immediately shut off. She scrambled to break free from the comforter as she heard the glass door on the shower stall open.

"Amber?"

"I'm fine!" She gave the comforter a vicious kick before running towards the door and her room. She was not getting caught naked by Joe this morning! The day was going to be tough enough without that little disadvantage.

Joe listened to the frantic paddle of bare feet on his wood floor and frowned. He ducked back under the showerhead and gave the handle a twist to wash the shampoo out of his hair. He didn't like her running out of his room. In fact, his pride was stinging as he heard the thump of the guestroom door as it slammed shut.

He gave the controls another twist and stepped out of the stall. Ripping a towel off the rack he applied it to his body. The mirror showed him a harsh expression. Too bad. Little Red and he needed to get a couple of things straight. She'd enjoyed herself in his bed and if she wanted to deny that he was more than willing to feed her her words again.

She was not going to run away from his bed.

His pager let out a shrill signal making him cuss. Goddamn it! Of all the stinking lousy timing! He grabbed the thing and looked at the line of code displayed on its screen.

Another round of profanity hit the mirror as he grabbed a clean uniform. Looked like his pride was going to have to get a number and wait in line.

* * * * *

Amber breathed a sigh of relief. She watched Joe back out of the driveway from her bathroom window. She had listened to him walk into her room and try the bathroom door. Her sudden streak of cowardice wasn't sitting on her stomach very well but she shook it off.

Tonight was going to be plenty soon enough to face the man. For that matter, she had no idea what hours Joe kept. Maybe he came home for lunch.

She took her shower at light speed. The water was near freezing because she'd let all the hot water run down the drain while watching the driveway. She muttered under her breath as her muscles cramped in the frigid liquid.

She cuddled inside a thick towel as she flung open the bathroom door. She froze as she looked at her desk chair. It was sitting exactly two feet in front of the doorway with its back facing the bathroom doorway. A stark white piece of printer paper was taped to its back. In bright red marker, Joe had left her a note.

Good morning, Honey, I'll be back.

Today suddenly looked like a great day to move to Idaho.

* * * * *

Amber worked instead. Her email box was crammed with urgent projects and rush jobs. Telecommuting held a whole lot of advantages—no office to report to, the ability to adjust her work hours around life's crises—but there was also the downside. Namely, people seemed to assume that if they sent a request to her before they left their office for the day, she would have it back to them when they arrived the next morning. Since she was dealing with every time zone on the planet, it was an impossible task.

Well, no job was perfect but hers was pretty good. In fact, today she was enjoying the mind-numbing, frantic pace that kept her from investigating her nocturnal behavior.

Amber finally pushed away from her desk when her hunger refused to wait any longer. Walking towards the kitchen, she sure hoped there was some of Deborah's casserole left in the refrigerator.

The microwave was humming along when the door opened. A little frown twisted her lips as Amber thought about facing Joe on an empty stomach. Solid footfalls came towards the kitchen making her frown. Joe was as light-footed as they came. These were heavy steps.

There was a flash of tan in the doorway as a man stepped into it. His eyes lit onto her as he gave a satisfied grunt. He was wearing the same uniform that Joe did but a soft belly pushed the lower part of it out.

"I'm Deputy Wilcox. The sheriff ordered me to bring you into town."

Joe could have done that. Amber looked at the man in front of her again, something wasn't right. Her eyes roamed over that uniform top before she found the place where a badge should have been. Instead there was nothing. Fear tightened her skin as it heightened her senses. There were multiple red welts covering the man's bare forearms.

"Those bees are persistent, aren't they?"

He nodded agreement before his face twisted into a frown. Amber lifted Deborah's casserole dish from the counter and heaved the thing at his head. She didn't wait to see if she hit her target. She sprinted out through the laundry room and slammed the door behind her.

Her fingers slipped on the lock as she frantically tried to bolt the door. Cussing filtered through, making her force the lock into place. She turned and shrieked as another man lowered his arms around her. She dropped to the floor and slipped right between his legs. The door gave a violent rumble as it was kicked from the kitchen side.

Pushing to her feet, she grabbed the open box of laundry detergent sitting on the washing machine and tossed the powder into the face of her nearest assailant.

"You goddamn bitch!"

The door splintered while the second man swiped at his white-covered face and cussed. Amber threw her body out the back door and towards the yard's dense landscaping. She was hauled right out of her tracks by a giant of a man who squeezed her rib cage until she heard the faint cracking of her bones.

"You two are a pair of fuck-ups."

"Damn bitch threw soap in my eyes!"

The man holding her squeezed her tighter as he laughed at her victim.

"So what? She's a redhead, they're always spicy. If the boss lets us have any fun with her, I get her first because I caught her. Got it?"

A large hand covered her face. Wet cloth was pressed to her nose and mouth as Amber struggled to get away from the sickening odor coming from it. The hand held as her vision blurred. Her body lost its grip on reality as her brain went black.

Chapter Eight

Amber didn't answer the house phone. Joe frowned as he listened to it ring. Punching in her cell phone number, he waited for her voice to answer. Instead her voice mail caught the call.

Dropping the phone, he stared at it. She could be ignoring him. Looking at his computer, he checked the online massager service she used. She'd turn as red as her hair if she found out he'd nosed through her laptop that morning.

Her laptop was idle. Pushing away from his desk, Joe headed for the door. He didn't like the feeling that was creeping down his neck. His gut instinct had saved his skin more than once and he wasn't going to ignore it.

* * * * *

Her head felt too heavy for her neck to hold up. Amber tried to lift her eyelids and found the task almost unbearable. She forced her eyes to open and moaned softly as light speared straight into her brain like a knife. Nausea gripped her stomach and she frantically tried to fend it off. A strip of fabric was tied around her head, gagging her.

Holy Christ!

She blinked and the room came into focus. She was tied to a chair in a very small kitchen. The single window had a blanket tossed over the curtain rod. Her feet were tied to each front leg of the chair while her hands were secured behind her.

Oh dear God, she had never been in this bad before. Her eyes flew around the kitchen as she tried to force her brain to think. Bad luck was one thing, this was life-threatening! The walls vibrated as voices filled the room just beyond the doorway. Her heart pounded frantically as she tried to concoct any sort of plan.

A solid, heavy step hit the floor and she let her head drop back to her chest. Another step hit the floor in the doorway as she tried to make her breathing even. A male grunt hit her ears before she heard those heavy footfalls moving away from her.

Opening a single eye, Amber looked at the doorway. She took even breaths as she forced her mind to resist the urge to panic. She had to figure a way out of this. Where there was the will, there was always a way.

And she had one hell of a will!

* * * * *

Joe wasn't mad. He knew the difference between anger and stone-cold rage. It burned along his body, releasing him from any form of guilt. All that was left was the instinct to hunt and destroy.

The phone rang and he grabbed it before half the ring tone had sounded.

"Lott."

"Boy, I'm sending you my best men." His uncle's voice might have sounded promising to anyone that didn't really know him. Joe heard the slight ring of resentment in it. The odds were almost insurmountable in kidnapping cases.

"Forget it, I've got it covered."

There was silence on the phone line. His uncle wasn't an armchair warrior. The man knew what the sting of battle tasted like. He also understood the code of silence that went with it.

"I didn't hear you, Josiah. The line is full of static and you're breaking up."

"Thank you, sir." Joe dropped the phone and looked at the team of investigators logging details in his house. Lifting his wrist he noted the time. He didn't need any witnesses when his team showed up.

Navy SEALs never broke up, even retirement from active duty just meant they went into deeper cover. Dantrolp had just made a mistake that gave Joe a reason to bring his team out of the woods. That little twist of his gut had been correct. The splintered door to his laundry room screamed at his own lack of complete trust in that warning. He should never have left Amber alone.

Joe just might let the man live long enough to regret what he'd done.

* * * * *

"When is that bitch going to wake up? You gave her too much of that shit."

"Oh yeah? Well, at least I didn't let a little pussy get the jump on me." Something crashed to the floor as there was a scuffling of feet. "Should have used that shit on you instead. I would be enjoying the day a lot more with her, that's for damn sure."

The front door slammed and the kitchen window vibrated. Another round of scuffling sounded from the front room before the window shook again with a second slamming of that door.

Amber lifted her head to renew her searching of the meager kitchen. She had no idea if there was anyone left in the outer room, but time was running out. Now that the effect of whatever drug they'd given her was completely gone, her brain was working.

There was a telephone sitting right on the counter, just four feet away. Olive-green, the thing looked left over from the eighties. Her captors certainly didn't put much faith in any ability she might have to outwit them. Her ankles were tied to the legs of the chair but her feet were sitting on the floor. There was nothing binding her waist to the chair. She could lift her bottom right out of it.

Looking at the phone, Amber flexed her hips away from the chair and back into it. The thing rocked with her motion so she did it again and again until it tipped forward on its front legs. She landed on her feet with the chair balanced on her back. It was an awkward position that made her hold still while she steadied her muscles.

Using her ankles, she took a tiny jump forward. The chair on her back bounced into her spine making her eyes smart with tears. She bit into the thin gag and jumped again. The wooden chair smacked her again as she forced her feet to jump again and again.

Tears streamed down her checks when she reached the counter. Looking at the face of the phone she searched for the function keys.

God did love her!

The speakerphone feature was on the bottom of the unit. A nice wide, square button—all she had to do was push it. Looking at the counter, she strained against the wood strapped to her back. The gag in her mouth was thin. Clamping her teeth tightly she could close her front teeth too.

A single pen was lying on the tile, stretching her neck she tried to grab it with her teeth. The effort had her almost panting but she clamped her jaw shut as the plastic tube hit her lips.

Amber worked the pen deeper into her mouth with her lips. It was a painfully slow process that had her fearing discovery any second. She finally bit into the thing with every last bit of strength in her jaw. Angling her weapon at the phone she stabbed at the button.

A dial tone filled the air as she frantically stabbed at the volume button. The dial tone died away as she fought to get high enough to punch in a phone number. Her spine screamed as she battled against the wooden chair, but she refused to let the pain defeat her.

Everything happened for a reason in life. She panted through her teeth as she punched the last digit of Joe's cell phone. She wasn't even sure why she memorized those contact numbers he'd given her.

Today she was certain it had been divine intervention that made her commit the information to her memory.

She let the pen drop from her teeth and began the slow journey away from the phone. Leaving the line open was the only thing she could think of doing. The gag was tied tight across her tongue.

The walls shook as the front door opened and her captor stomped back into the house. Amber dropped the chair to the floor and sat in it. She was only halfway back to her original position but she didn't dare get caught moving.

"Well, would you look at that. You sure are pretty."

She swallowed the nausea his words inspired. Amber choked on the gag and struggled to breathe. He chuckled at her distress and flipped open a pocketknife.

"Can't have you strangling just yet."

Amber sucked in a huge lungful of air as she spat the gag out of her mouth. Her tongue screamed with pain as its binding was released. She choked and gasped before tossing her hair out of her face. With any luck, the phone line was still open.

"Where am I?"

"You don't need to know."

The second man appeared in the doorway and smirked at her. Amber felt the blood drain from her face as his eyes traveled over every inch of her body. He lingered on her spread thighs before he rubbed his crotch.

The ties on her wrists held as she strained against them. Her brain suddenly filled with anger as she watched a smile contort her captor's face. He rubbed his crotch again and smirked as he did it. Amber pointedly looked at his fly before raising a bored expression to his face.

"You really don't want to try any of that with me."

He spat on the floor. "I'll do whatever the hell I want. Boss is going to waste you anyway."

"You are full of it." Amber tossed her head and looked at the first man. His eyes didn't hold the delight that the one in the doorway did. But his expression sent a chill down her back. The idea of her death sat on his face without remorse.

"Well, then you'd really better not piss me off."

"What the fuck do you mean?"

Amber clamped her emotion under iron control. The only weapon she had was her brain and she was betting her life on being able to outwit these two thugs. She forged towards the battle with a smile on her face.

"My mother is a voodoo master. She'll curse you so damn bad, you'll beg for death like a baby. She does it all — black magic, Cajun curses and stuff you never heard of."

"Bullshit!"

Amber laughed as she saw the smallest hint of apprehension enter his face. His hand had stopped rubbing his genitals and now lay like a shield over the bulge in his pants.

"She lives right outside New Orleans. Right next to the graveyard. Did you enjoy those killer bees? How about that hurricane? See, she's mad at me for leaving her home. She cursed me with bad luck until I came back to her."

They both looked worried now. It wasn't a matter of believing her, it was more a point of not taking the chance of her being right.

"Then I get hit with a bag of cocaine? Oh, please! Now kidnapping? It's a curse. I ran away from her magic." Amber forced her body to shiver. "You should have seen what she did to her last boyfriend. He cheated on her and she made sure he'd never do it again — ever."

"Put that damn gag back in her fucking mouth!"

"Yeah."

The giant scooped up the gag and tied it back around her head. Amber glared at him but shook with relief. Both men wanted to get away from her.

"She's full of shit." With the gag in place, the man in the doorway seemed to muster his courage. His eyes moved over her as he gave his crotch a hard rub.

"Maybe." The giant lifted his arm to stare at his bee stings. His eyes lifted to her before he moved away from her. "I don't need a piece of ass bad enough to test out her words. That voodoo shit is serious stuff. That was one of the biggest beehives I've ever seen. Enough drones in that thing to kill a man. Nope. No pussy poke is worth that."

He left, shouldering the man in the doorway aside as he went. Another rub to his crotch and the second man spat on the floor before leaving the kitchen. The little room got darker as the sun set. Her limbs cramped and her mouth begged for water but Amber kept her ears tightly tuned for any sound that her reprieve from molestation was over. The television was on in the other room. A basketball game held the attention of her captors as she cast a longing look at the telephone.

Fatigue was taking its toll. Her body became one single point of pain. Her spine hurt from her walk across the floor. The fabric of her gag seemed to be wicking every bit of moisture away from her mouth and even her throat. The darkness closed in as she found herself looking at the light shining in from the outer room as a friend.

The muffled sound of the television began to take on a comforting feeling. A cold draft of night air hit her bare arms. Turning her head she bit even harder into the gag as the shadows behind her grew and moved. She wasn't even sure they were men, they merged with the darkness too completely.

Every inch of them was hard and deadly. Their gazes moving over her with razor-sharp precision. Pistols leading the way, they dismissed her and closed in on the men in the next room.

It was all completely silent.

A solid hand wrapped around her head making her jump. Her head landed against a hard chest before the man slipped to one knee behind her. His lips stopped just a single millimeter from her ear. A low shush was the only sound he made. The muzzle of another gun appeared in his opposite hand, aimed towards the doorway.

The two men at the door waited. Their bodies were a study in control. So, strong yet not tense as they held their guns steady. Their reason for halting arrived two seconds later when the front door exploded into kindling. The men coming through it fired off several rounds as they converged on her captors.

"Clear!"

The same word bounced out of each man's chest including the one holding her. A second later she was free. The rope on her ankles slit with an efficient slice of a wicked-looking blade. Her hands sprang apart after one more swipe of that same knife.

Amber reached for her gag but her hands refused to perform. Instead her arms quivered in jerks in her lap. The gag sailed towards the floor as two hands appeared on her arms and began a rough massage of her aching limbs.

"Well now, I hope someone got shot. They had you tied up way too long. You are gonna hurt like hell tomorrow morning."

Her tongue refused to work as well. The outer room was silent. It was an eerie end to the nightmare. So quick and quiet, somehow, she just couldn't wrap her mind around the concept that it was really over.

The light from the outer room dimmed as a body stepped into the doorway. Even covered from head to toe in black, she knew who it was. Every cell in her body recognized Joe. It happened on an instinctive level.

His boots hardly made contact with the floor as he approached. The hands working on her muscles disappeared as he bent his knee and lowered his head to eye level with her. His face was covered in black makeup of some kind. Even his lips were covered with it. The eyes that inspected her were almost foreign to her.

Every civilized mannerism was stripped away. She stared at the iron-hard truth that she'd only suspected Joe held inside him. He waited for her to see it. His eyes watched the realization dawn on her. A slow nod was her approval.

He ran a firm hand over her quivering legs. She wanted out of that chair so bad, yet her body failed to give her the strength to even rise under her own strength. Blood was making a slow, agonizing path back down to her feet.

The strength she suspected was in his body materialized as he simply lifted her from the chair. She landed against this chest as his arms cradled her.

Being in contact with his flesh sent of a wave of relief so great her conscious mind simply shut down as it hit. There didn't seem to be any reason to struggle anymore. Faith and trust merged with her relief, making it impossible to ignore the need to surrender to exhaustion.

Her head hit his shoulder as Amber collapsed. Joe let his rage free as he crossed over the bound bodies of her captors. Facedown on the carpet, they were hogtied and gagged.

He didn't spare them a second glace. His team would get around to hauling them off to a more secure location. Amber was his concern now.

The night air was crisp. It emphasized the warm brush of Amber's respiration hitting his neck. He savored the feeling as he continued on to a Hummer that had pulled into the yard after they'd penetrated the structure.

Second-rate scum. They were the soft kind who never really dealt with true battle. Idiots like that were used to surrendering and getting a lawyer to defend them when they screwed up a job.

Joe had hoped they'd give him an excuse to fire on them. Disappointment flooded him as he gently let Amber roll onto the rear seat of the Hummer. Her body was limp and chilled as shock set in. He yanked a trauma blanket out of the seat back and tucked the silver edges around her body.

He smoothed the red curls back from her face a second before sealing her inside the vehicle. Deep satisfaction flooded his body as he watched his team load their cargo onto the flatbed of another Hummer.

SEALs were known for their effectiveness—not their hospitality.

Dirt flew up from the tires as they quit the scene as quickly as they'd taken it.

Chapter Nine

"You could just kill me quickly, you know!!"

A soft male chuckle was her answer. Amber glared at the man responsible for that sound. She knew it on a subatomic level now. A pair of amused eyes watched her fume from her padded prison.

A place that was also known as her bed. Two solid days of confinement and she couldn't take it anymore! She glared at the SEAL Joe called Snip and kicked the bedding aside. His face lost its grin and a bit of its color too.

"Now behave, Ms. Talisman. Chief would skin me if I had to tussle with you."

She was counting on that fact too. Joe had set his buddies to watching her and they did it with perfection. They even followed her to the bathroom. She was never alone. Their muscle-packed shoulders were always in sight as were their guns.

Black, deadly looking pistols. They were tucked into waistbands and sometimes shoulder harnesses but she hadn't seen a single male since her rescue who didn't have a weapon clearly displayed. She was beginning to wonder just who was expected to see the firepower—her kidnappers or herself.

Joe called it protective custody. Somehow, Amber got the feeling this was a little more than the normal brand of that service. These men wouldn't just defend her, they intended to kill anyone that even flinched in her direction.

Their vigil had given her the space to sleep but now it was chafing. Her life was always full of conflict, and adopting hiding as a defense wasn't going to happen as long as there was breath in her lungs.

"I need exercise, Snip. Give me a break, I just want to try a little walking."

"Doc said three days bed rest."

She hissed and crawled onto all fours. Her fanny was numb from being in bed for two days. All right, so maybe the rest of her body was screaming from every movement she made but she would get up!

"I bet the Chief you wouldn't stay in bed for three days without being tied to it." Snip clamped his mouth shut as he heard his own words. "Hell, no...ah...I meant..."

"You meant what you said."

Amber grinned at the man's slip before taking another deep breath and swinging her feet over the side of the bed.

Her feet hit the floor and her legs erupted with pain. Amber gritted her teeth and forced her body up off the bed's surface. She was getting up! Right now! Snip groaned under his breath before aiming all two hundred pounds of his muscled frame at her.

"I got her, Snip. Take a break."

The man stopped exactly three feet in front of her. His eyes mirrored relief as he suddenly grinned at her. Amber felt the color leave her face. That hadn't been a friendly sort of grin, it was the kind you gave somebody when you knew they were going to catch a ration of hell.

Snip moved aside to show her Joe. His hands were tucked into his waistband as his face reflected his determination to bend her to his will.

And that wasn't an exaggeration either.

How did you go to bed with a man and never really know what he was? The man who stood in front of her had dropped his civilian camouflage. It was like seeing the fangs on a rattlesnake for the first time. Somehow, she'd convinced herself that Joe was just a cop and that kind of man she could handle. Sure, he carried a gun, but his basic mode of operation was capture and containment of scumbags, not devour and destroy.

Her stomach made a nervous flop in her belly as she considered the hard glitter of his eyes. The tingling sensation crossing her bottom as blood circulation was restored tightened her resolve. Need moved through her body like a theme song as her eyes traced his shoulders. It was an immediate reaction to him. One that happened the second Joe walked into her line of sight.

Idaho…

"I am getting out of bed." Amber moved away from the edge of the mattress and those black eyes snapped at her. Amber bit her lip as her arms sent out a painful wail.

"Amber, stop being so stubborn. You need to rest."

"What I want is to get out of this room." She wasn't going to win the need question. Joe had doctors backing him up. She shifted her weight between her feet as she tested her legs for stability. After a day tied up, her muscles were like noodles that refused to respond to her commands.

"I mean it, Joe. I need to get up! Stop treating me like a baby." Amber pushed her feet forward two steps despite the twinges of pain racing along her muscles. "It's not that bad! Besides, a little exercise just might loosen the whole mess up."

He wasn't treating her like a baby. Joe never had seen her as anything but a woman. But he was taking her confinement as the chance to avoid certain issues. Small beads of sweat shimmered on her forehead as she forced her legs to move. The pain wasn't unbearable and he had to admire her tenacity. Her spunk had always impressed him.

That didn't mean she had what it took to accept him. Truth was most women didn't. They fantasized about having a real live alpha man, but when faced with one they ran for the nearest apron-holding mama's boy they could twist around their whims.

Just letting the idea that Amber might want to run away cross his brain made him want to dissolve into complete revolt. Her leaving wasn't an option as far as he was concerned. Not now and possibly not ever. Those drops of water on the side of her face touched his pride with how much spunk she really had. It seeped into his brain and hit some dark spot where a man thought about a woman in the most primitive way. Amber was the female he wanted to see his baby growing inside of. He wanted to kill any male who looked at her the same way and his cock was rock-hard just thinking about pumping another load of his seed inside of her.

"See? Just fine and dandy."

Joe grunted and crossed his arms across his chest. The posture was ultra-male. It pricked her pride with its complete superiority but it also touched that deep part of her that turned on anytime Joe looked at her with his sharp eyes. The part of her that had clung to him when all rational thought shredded and she tried to hold him between her open thighs.

"I think that tremor working down your legs is going to drop you on that sassy bottom in about three minutes."

"Sassy?"

Her cheeks turned as red as her hair. Amber choked that one word out in a squeak while her hands tightened into little fists. It was the honest truth that her temper made him itch. His cock rose to immediate attention as he watched her emotions bleed over her porcelain skin.

"Oh yeah, honey, first thing I noticed about you was that sassy seat. It makes me hard just looking at it."

"I am not your honey!" She worked her shoulders back and forth with her words. Her fists were propped onto her hips making her breasts jiggle with her temper. Joe clenched his teeth together as his jeans became painfully tight. In another ten seconds, he'd be imposing those doctor's orders just for the joy of putting her back into that bed. Only she wouldn't be going alone.

Joe captured her body with one solid arm around her waist. She sputtered as her head tipped back to point her fuming gaze at him. He stroked the side of her face as he cupped one side of her bottom to keep her from curling her hips away from his. He wanted her to feel the swollen erection she'd inspired in him. Watching her eyes turn glassy with desire soothed the need pounding in his blood to restate his claim on her.

She suddenly ached in a completely different way. The pain of her abused limbs was nothing compared to the yearning erupting inside her body. The walls of her passage felt so empty. The hard promise of his body tempting her to once again forget any form of thought. Instead, to embrace her yearnings and the man who had proven his ability to satisfy her.

"You are a lot of things to me, honey." Her eyes flashed as she squirmed against his hold. Joe controlled her movements before lowering his head until their breath mingled. His fingers caught the back of her head and kept her in place.

"Just as soon as you recover, we can get back to playing traffic games."

His mouth thrust her denial right back into her throat. Amber listened to her own moan of weakness even as she frantically tried to muster some form of resistance. Instead her tongue went to meet his. Twisting and stroking the length of his as her lips opened to completely surrender to his kiss. Her body surged forward towards the hard length of his cock. Wanting it closer. Needing it to fill the empty walls that were heating and moistening in welcome for him.

Her feet left the ground and she wound her arms around his shoulders. Their mouths still mingled as he took her back to the bed that suddenly seemed like the most important destination she had ever had.

"How about a hot bath?"

A little moan of approval escaped her lips before she clamped her jaw shut. His eyes lit up with enjoyment, making her simmer.

"There's a hot tub out back, you can try some exercise in it. Agreed?"

Her body shouted approval but her pride struggled against letting him see it. Just exactly why was it the man seemed to be able to read her so well? It was extremely annoying. He was so brutally male, it would be nice to think of him as a male creature that couldn't possibly understand a woman's needs.

Instead he offered her a delight that any female would have lavished attention on him for suggesting. It was stuff like that that made her heart melt. How did you plan to move to Idaho when there was a man heating up a hot tub just for you?

"It sounds great."

"You know, honey, some women like being looked after."

Amber shot him a harassed look and rolled her eyes. "Maybe I should start acting like one. I bet that would bore you in one-hour flat."

Her mouth was her worst enemy! Amber groaned as Joe's eyes lit with amusement.

"You understand me better than I thought." His eyes went somber as he considered her. Deep consideration watched her from his dark eyes. It was almost like he was looking right into her soul. Her eyes were glued to his as she looked right back and found him letting her look at him for a change.

He let her feet down but held a solid arm around her waist. The water was already hot and bubbly. A little mutter of delight slipped out of her mouth as she sat on the edge of the tub and dipped her bare feet into the warm water.

Joe couldn't help but grin as he watched her. She played with the bubbles before kicking her feet in the foam. Her face was radiant as her eyes sparkled and little giggles came through her lips. She pushed off the edge of the tub and right into the water in her pajamas. The tank top and short set instantly turned transparent where the water hit the fabric. Amber didn't take the time to notice, she was too busy being happy.

This was so much better than her bed! Amber felt her body loosen up and her blood start flowing through her veins again. It was like her entire circulatory system had been limping along with huge lumps flowing through it. She rolled her shoulders and sank down in the water to let the heat work on the knot sitting over her spine where the chair had hit it.

A male foot stepped into the tub and she looked up to discover Joe joining her in the hot water. Her lips pressed together as she stared at the magnificent example of manhood he displayed without a single stitch of clothing on his body. Dark curly hair covered his chest and his abdomen where his cock stood out from his body in blunt display. She just couldn't help but look at that swollen rod. The large head was ruby red with a small drop of fluid sitting in its slit. He lowered his second foot and it bounced before Joe sat down and his cock disappeared beneath the water. Amber jerked her eyes up to his face to find him watching her. He suddenly laughed at her.

"I love the way you blush."

Well, she hated it! The damn habit turned her face the same shade as her hair and even if a person was color-blind, she doubted they'd miss her face changing shades. Snip moved past the patio, making her eyes widen as she realized that Joe's team of cloak-and-dagger action men were currently watching them.

"What are you doing in here?" Her hands fluttered as she tried to think of a way to state the most pressing part of her concern. "Ah...like that?"

"Like what? You referring to me being naked, bare, maybe even raw?"

Amber shoved her hands in the water and sent a wave of it at his face. It hit him right across his nose but he shook his head and grinned at her. "Your friends are watching us!"

"They'd better be, the governor isn't paying them to sit on their seats."

"But you're naked."

His lips twitched as he lowered his torso into the water and groaned with appreciation for the hot water. "Trust me, Amber, they know what a cock looks like."

Well, fine! He was telling her she was being ridiculous, and in a really testosterone sort of way she supposed he was right. Didn't guys all have some kind of locker room code that said seeing each other in the buff was just manly? "Sorry, I forgot that women have manners, that's all."

Joe leaned against the side of the hot tub and let his eyes trace her blush again. "Honey, if you think a wooden door masks all those little sexy sounds you make, you're wrong. My men would know exactly what we were doing."

"I am not into public displays." Oooh, but the idea made her nipples tingle. Her body surged with ideas that bordered on taboo as her mind flatly refused to consider changing her decisions. But her eyes roamed over his chest and the ridges of muscle sitting so close to her fingertips. Her memory decided to replay the image of him stepping down into the tub and the hard erection he was hiding beneath the foaming surface.

The things her mind chose to remind her that that erection did to her, made her body shiver before she felt fluid rushing to her passage. Jesus! Somehow, giving in to the urge to have sex with Joe made it impossible for her to ignore any further impulses about him and his hard body. The cock hidden by the hot tub bubbles made her weak as she thought about how simple it would really be to take a little step and reach out until her fingers curled around its hard length.

Ohh…and it would be hard too. Her fingertips would tell her exactly how delightful that stiff flesh would feel slipping up into her body as the hot water swirled around them.

"You could burn me with those eyes, baby."

Her lips formed a round expression of surprise right before Amber took a jerky step away from him. She slipped on the bottom of the smooth fiberglass tub and went towards the ground. Joe plucked her up just before her head went under the bubbles.

Amber listened to her own moan and for once didn't blush. She had been so right! His cock was hard beneath the bubbles and it burned into her belly making her snap her teeth together to hold back a whimper. Her hands smoothed over his chest as she refused to keep her fingers away from his skin. He just felt so damn good!

Joe's lips brushed her neck before stopping next to her ear. His hands moved over her bottom as that hard cock burned against her. "Games can be a whole lot of fun, baby. Right here, I could slip into that tight little body of yours and see how long you could keep your lips closed." One of his hands gripped her thigh and lifted it. His cock slipped between her open legs and lay against her burning sex. There was nothing between them but some wet fabric and temptation screamed at her to take a wild chance and just give in to Joe's words.

His mouth caught hers as she struggled to get closer to him. His arms held her solidly against him as she felt his hands stroke her bottom and press her hips towards his cock.

"Easy, baby. I don't really care but I bet you might if I took you right here."

Her eyes were dazed with desire as Joe savored the soft cheeks of her bottom sitting in his hands. His cock raged with the knowledge that she was bare under her little pajama shorts, all he had to do was push the fabric aside to touch her pussy. He wanted to — God! He wanted to fuck her right then and make sure every man on his team heard her cry out as he pleasured her.

He was an animal but fought against the urge to demonstrate it so publicly.

His arms caught her up and his body rose out of the water in the same motion. Amber landed against his chest as he carried her out of the hot tub and back towards the bed she'd been so determined to leave. Now it looked inviting with the door that could be closed to keep the rest of the world away.

Joe walked right past the guestroom. He let her feet slip to the floor as one of his hands stripped her wet shirt over her head. It hit the wood floor with a soft squish as his hands cupped her breasts. Pleasure hummed across her skin as he gently massaged the sensitive globes.

A shadow crossed the window behind Amber, and Joe let his mouth curve into a grin. She didn't need to know that his men had taken notice of just what he was up to. Nope, it wasn't a romantic idea but it was very enjoyable. It was primitive, just as basic as his need to get inside her body. Her slim fingers suddenly curled around his cock making his breath rasp between his teeth.

"See, honey?"

"You need a warning label, Joe Lott." Amber trembled as she stroked the hard length of his cock. Lord help her, the thing felt delicious against her hand. Wicked little ideas paraded across her mind as she considered returning a few of the favors he'd shown her during their first traffic lesson.

"So, Josiah, how's your tolerance for yellow lights?" Amber wiggled out of her wet pajama bottoms before flashing him a view of her sassy seat. She climbed onto his bed and crawled across it on all fours. Joe growled with appreciation as she lifted one hand and crocked a finger at him.

"Come over here, Josiah."

She lowered her belly to the bed and propped her elbows on the mattress. Her little toes wiggled in the air as she bent her knees and kicked her feet into the air. Joe watched her finger as it beckoned him closer. His cock jerked as he stepped forward and she slipped her fingers around him again.

Her lips stopped a bare inch from the head of his cock as she aimed her eyes at his face. "Oh, you didn't answer me, Josiah. Aren't you Navy SEALs taught to say, yes, ma'am?"

His fingers twisted in her hair as he growled at her. Amber giggled and smoothed her hand down the length of his erection. Her own body burned with need but she was having fun too, and the combination was euphoric.

"Suck me." His words were hard and demanding but they sounded delightful to her. Amber sent her hand down his cock again as his fingers tightened on her hair. "Close enough."

Her little tongue licked the head of his cock and he groaned. She licked all the way around the head with no hurry. Her wet tongue found the slit in the top of his cock and tormented it before circling the head again.

"Yes, I seem to remember you showing me exactly how long a yellow light could last for."

Oh shit!

Amber lowered her head until she captured the top of his length. She closed her lips around him and listened to the hiss his breath made as he sucked it in. That little male sound pushed her forward with confidence as she relaxed her jaw and took more of his cock into her mouth. Her tongue found the spot right under the head where all her girlfriends had said you could drive a man crazy by rubbing it. Joe's hands twisted in her hair as she sucked and licked together.

"Jesus, baby! That feels so damn good!"

His hands urged her forward and Amber didn't disappoint him. The scent from his body drove her towards wringing more harsh male sounds from his mouth. She sent her fingers down the remaining length of his cock as she licked and sucked harder. His cock suddenly jerked as her hand cupped the twin sacs beneath his rod. A harsh cry hit her ears as his seed hit her tongue. His hand was rigid as it held her head in place. Amber didn't care, she was delighted by the eruption in her mouth. She licked and sucked on his cock as she listened to him suck in a huge gasp of air and pant as pleasure shook his body.

"Maybe I should have let your men see that."

Joe growled at her. Amber rose up on all fours and pushed back to her knees. His face was harsh but his eyes latched onto her breasts. She wasn't sure why she wanted to bait him, but the idea refused to stop tempting her with dark pictures of the man she'd seen in his eyes when he'd rescued her from that kitchen.

Lifting her hands, she gently played with her own nipples. "You stepped into that hot tub naked to prove a point to your buddies, didn't you?" Amber ran one hand down her chest and over her belly as she looked at the hard cock still standing up from his body. Lifting her eyes, she looked into the harsh demand burning from his eyes.

"Maybe I should let them see that you respond to me, too."

A low laugh met her remark. His hand gently stroked the side of her face before Joe joined her on the bed. His men did know exactly what they were doing but he suddenly understood that Amber didn't need to know that. She was a sweet garden growing in between the harsh streets of the ugly world. He cupped her breast and watched her eyes fill with pleasure. His woman wasn't for display.

"You drive me insane, honey, and I think it's time to return the favor."

Her breath caught in her throat as Joe smoothed his hand down her belly. A little shiver shook her body as he followed his hand. Her thighs parted for him as he gently smoothed the folds of her sex. "In fact, Amber, I think I might enjoy playing lots of different kinds of games with you. We'll have to try out a few others beside red light, green light."

Her eyes flew open as he settled between her spread thighs. Joe watched her as he slipped one finger between the slick flesh. "Now, where were we? Ah, yellow light."

His mouth caught her and Amber groaned. The sound just rose from her chest as pleasure took complete command of her thoughts. His hands spread her open as his tongue targeted the little bud at the top of her slit. Pleasure so intense it bordered on pain shot up her body and then down again. Her womb contracted as Joe used one finger to gently penetrate her aching passage. Her hips bucked as she frantically tried to get closer to his tongue. Tension tightened until it broke and another low moan hit the afternoon.

"Oh baby, that was way too fast." One finger thrust into her body as he held her thighs open. "But I love the fact that sucking my cock turned you on that much."

The crude language hit her ears and made her even hotter. It wasn't that Amber liked profanity, but hearing the words used for what they really meant made her shiver. People said those same words all the time when they were mad, but hearing it on Joe's voice made her want to suck him off all over again.

"I love how wet you get for me." His eyes were watching his finger as he thrust it into her body. Pulling it free, Joe sent it along the ultrasensitive center of her slit until he found her clit. He pressed on the little button as Amber listened to her own whimper.

"Wet and sweet."

Her pussy glistened and Joe sent the tip of his tongue over her clit. Her hips bucked as he used one arm to brace her against the surface of the bed. Sucking her bud between his lips, he sent two fingers into her pussy as he listened to her moan. It was the sexiest sound a woman ever made. She jerked but he held her down and lapped her slit before pressing his fingers into her again. Raising his eyes, Joe looked up her body to the tight nipples that crowned her breasts. Her back was arched as he thrust into her again.

His mouth sucked her clit and Amber let insanity take her. She went willingly as her body jerked and bounced on waves of pleasure. It all centered on Joe's mouth as he sucked and lapped at her. He didn't let her climax, instead he would stop sucking on her clit just before the tension broke into release.

"Joe, please!"

His fingers thrust deeply into her as her body reached a painful level of need. "Hmm, what was that comment you made about answering up, baby? Maybe you just need to ask me for what you want."

Amber's eyes flew open as Joe circled her clit with his finger. Climax simmered like a mirage but she couldn't reach it because his arm held her completely still on the bed. Those hard eyes watched her face as he ran that finger down her slit and circled the opening to her body with it.

"Tell me to make you come, baby." His finger thrust into her body making her frantic for more than just one finger. She needed to be stretched around his cock. Filled with the hard flesh that she could see. His eyes glittered as his jaw drew tight against his own needs. "I won't fuck you until you tell me to eat this pussy."

He meant it too. Amber whimpered as his fingers rubbed over her clit again. Hearing those words was one thing, but what kind of girl talked like that? But she wanted what he promised. Oh God, she didn't want to have sex, she wanted Joe to fuck her.

"Eat me, Joe."

She whispered the words but Joe didn't make her beg. His head dropped to her spread body and instantly renewed their attention over her clit. Her body jerked as he gave her enough pressure to climax.

Joe growled with her harsh cry. Her hips bucked as she tore at his hair and he savored every millisecond of it. Giving one last lap to her clit he rose onto his knees. The spread flesh of her body glistened with her climax. Need tore into his cock as he pulled her hips towards him and thrust into her body. The tight walls of her passage gripped his cock, making him grunt. The need to get inside her body became more intense every time he had his cock inside her. Instead of sating his appetite, fucking her only fueled it.

"I love hearing you talk dirty to me, baby."

Joe wanted to control her this time. Amber looked into his face and saw the raw need flashing back at her. His hands held her hips as he sat on his haunches. His hips flexed and thrust as he pulled her hips towards him.

"Put your hands above your head." Amber watched the possessive light enter his eyes before she lifted her hands to the pillows above her. Her breasts rose into twin mountains that his eyes latched onto while he thrust deeply between her thighs.

"You are stunning, baby." Amber stared at his face as a new emotion mixed with the light of possession. Somehow, the harsh expression of need mixed with a tender note of affection. It transformed the sex into intimacy as her body shivered and tightened for another climax.

"That's it, baby, come for me. Keep your eyes open, I want to watch it sparkle across those baby blues."

Her breath caught but her body refused to wait. Joe thrust deeply as she tumbled into climax and her passage gripped his cock. He felt the eruption of his seed as he pulled out and thrust even deeper into her. Her thighs grasped his hips as his seed splashed against the mouth of her womb.

Her body was useless. Amber couldn't have moved if she had to. Ripples of pleasure ran across her nerve endings as she tried to fill her lungs with enough air. Joe rolled onto the bed beside her and pulled her body next to his. She shouldn't have needed any more sleep, but with her head cushioned on his chest she dropped away into slumber.

Joe twisted one lock of red hair around his finger. His cock twitched as he felt a snarl escape his mouth. He wanted to flip her over and fuck her again and maybe even again but he didn't want to move as her little hand threaded through his chest hair. He was torn between tender and raw emotions but it all settled onto their bodies like glitter, making him grin.

"Sleep, baby. I'll be here when you wake up."

Chapter Ten

Amber glared at her mirror and hissed. She fluffed her hair and made sure the auburn curls were sitting in front of her shoulders today. Her eyes looked around the bathroom and noticed the little hints of its owner.

She shouldn't be so nervous. Just because she had never shared a man's room before didn't mean she should be...concerned. Women did it all the time.

She huffed on her way out the door. A shadow moved as Snip shifted out of his spot to allow her to move through the hallway. Her face went up in flames. She quickened her pace but Snip kept step with her.

Amber tried not to keep looking at the man. Her fingers shook as she filled a glass with ice and opened the door to the refrigerator for the pitcher of tea she'd made before her kidnapping. It wouldn't be very good but caffeine sounded delightful to her groggy system.

She turned with the pitcher and looked at Snip leaning against the kitchen counter. He looked at the doorway behind her before moving his eyes to the sliding glass door in front of him. The man had the same precise movement of his eyes that Joe did, but Amber didn't feel the radiation of strength from Snip. It wasn't that she doubted his ability to spring into action if needed, it just wasn't that overwhelming sense of power that seemed to hit her when she stood in a room with Joe.

What she did feel was surrounded. The leather shoulder harness buckled over his shirt glared at her as Snip moved his eyes around the kitchen once again.

"You've never been under protection before, have you, ma'am."

Snip wasn't asking her. The Navy SEAL stated it as fact. He suddenly moved and plucked the pitcher from her frozen hands before she realized he was reaching towards her. His dark brown eyes smiled at her as he filled her glass and handed the pitcher back to her.

"You'll get used to it, ma'am."

"No offense, but I sure hope not."

He nodded his head before running his eyes around the room again. He pushed away from the counter and moved to the opposite side of the kitchen.

"Chief went into town for a spell."

Snip's words made her sad. Amber suddenly felt like she was caught in a net while the rest of the world went on spinning without her. Joe had responsibilities to deal with and she had to just sit and wait until the creep with the cocaine showed up in court.

Alarm raced through her mind next as she considered the fact that she had no idea how long it took to get a trial date. She just might be a blithering idiot by the time Snip was relieved of his duty to shadow her.

Snip's eyes suddenly focused on her neck for a split second before a little flame of wicked amusement crossed his eyes and he looked back at the opposite doorway. Amber spun on her heel and headed for her computer. The warm afternoon air made her pout as she thought about the small purple bruises on her neck. She couldn't cover the things up with a turtleneck even if she wanted to. No one was going to believe she was cold. Besides, every man guarding her knew what she and Joe had been up to in the master bedroom.

Jesus! Why in the hell did little girls dream about being princesses? Being the center of absolute attention was the pits!

* * * * *

"Wrong bed."

Amber shrieked and fell into the bed in question. Hard and masculine, Joe's voice filled the guestroom like a bullhorn. Her reaction amused him. She saw the telltale flicker of humor cross his eyes even if the rest of his face was set into disapproving concrete.

"I was working but maybe I'll sleep right here if you're grumpy tonight."

Joe hooked his hands into his belt and glared at her. He was reading her with his eyes once again, as he looked at her system and then back. Amber felt her lips curl up into a grin. She had just powered down for the night so there wasn't any evidence for him to find. Her amusement was her downfall. His eyes targeted the expression before he ran a hand over the side of her laptop.

Amber pouted at him as he smiled. Her laptop would be warm and his fingers had found the heat.

"See? Rocking the boat."

Amber shrugged but couldn't help but smile. She lifted both her hands into the air. "Told you I was working. You're the one who fired off the accusation. You seemed to have a need to command."

Joe laughed low and deep as he nodded his head at her. "That's right, baby, and maybe we'll play with a few games that will change your mind about liking my orders…but save your teasing for my face…never sneak up on me."

Her face went serious as she thought about his words. Joe watched her as his mouth turned down into a frown. He needed to know she could take it. Him, the hard edges and the carefully constructed framework the rest of the world saw.

He suddenly frowned deeper as Snip's report filtered into his brain.

"Did your mother make you feel guilty for sleeping with me?"

Amber rolled her eyes at him. "Hardly." She bit her lower lip and regretted even that one word. Somehow, she didn't like the feeling that Joe might have a negative reaction to her mom. Now, Amber took her mom as she was, but a whole lot of people liked to judge.

"Does that mean she likes me?"

Trust Joe to pull out a shovel and dig no matter what danger signs might be posted around a subject. Maybe she should just pull her top off and change the subject. A naughty grin curled her lips as she thought about how Joe's eyes always seemed to latch onto her breasts. She'd never really thought too much about whether or not she was pretty. The way Joe looked at her made her feel stunning.

"Amber, if you're climbing into that bed because your mother called then give me her number because I've got a few things to say to her."

"Excuse me, I mentioned it because you sounded grumpy. Something must have kept you up last night."

His teeth flashed at her as he stepped into the room. "You like sleeping with me. In fact, you like it a whole lot. But it's the bedtime stories that you crave the most."

Her face flushed but her body nagged her to be brazen and just yank her pajamas off. The sight of her bare coral nipples would end this conversation right quickly! "Just because you like something doesn't mean you overindulge yourself."

"Give me your mother's number. I think it's time I introduced myself to her."

"That's not a good idea." Joe picked her cell phone up off the desk in response. His eyes made a brief scan of the screen before he began pushing commands into the little unit. Amber surged off the bed and made a grab for her phone.

She had no idea what she'd been thinking. One huge arm clamped her to Joe's side as he lifted her phone in the other hand and continued to search the memory for her mother's number.

"Give me that phone!"

"Nope." Joe shot her a determined look as he moved his hand to one side of her bottom. "If you want to let someone else into our relationship, honey, fine, but I have a few things to say about that too."

"I didn't let her into our relationship."

Joe grinned at her and Amber hit his shoulder. "That doesn't mean we are having a relationship either!"

"Then why don't you want me to talk to your mom?" He smacked her bottom and cupped it again. Amber squirmed but froze as she felt the unmistakable rise of his cock against her belly. It twitched and swelled as she felt her body hum with approval.

"There it is." Joe looked back at her phone and pressed the redial button. He was pushing the issue but it felt so important to understand why Amber wanted to keep any form of distance between them. There was something lurking in her eyes that looked like fear and fear had a way of building walls between people.

"Forget it, Joe. My mom thinks I should jump into your bed and enjoy myself."

Joe cut the call and dropped the phone back onto the desk. His arm came around her body and pulled her closer.

"Uh-oh, do I detect a son-in-law hunter?"

"No, not even close."

Joe lifted her off her feet and swung her against his chest. He angled her through the doorway and down the hallway.

Amber landed in the middle of the master bed. Her body instantly reminded her about their morning spent among the flannel sheets. Her face burned hotter as Joe studied her with his sharp eyes. That little grin appeared on her face again as she enjoyed the pure testosterone of the moment. A girl didn't need to ask if a man liked what he saw when that same man carried her off to his bed!

Her eyes suddenly noticed that Flamingo was in the corner of the room with a small space heater aimed at his shell.

"Oh!!! First cantaloupe and now a space heater? Stop bribing my tortoise!"

Joe grinned. It wasn't a nice kind of grin, it was a victory expression that made her temper boil. Amber glared at her pet. "See if I cut up cucumbers for you tomorrow." The reptile didn't even blink. Instead

Flamingo was completely at ease with his arms and legs hanging out of his shell. The posture meant he was warm and very happy. Looking back at Joe, Amber smirked.

"You know, Flamingo isn't housebroken."

Joe glared at Flamingo before raising one finger at the reptile. "You better be a good bunkmate, Frank. Now excuse me, I need to seduce your mama. All that sputtering you hear coming from her pretty red head says she's hot and bothered." Amber's eyes bulged as Joe looked back at her.

"I always check the details of a mission, baby. Bribing a tortoise isn't the hardest task I've undertaken to ensure success. Now explain why you think your mom isn't son-in-law hunting."

Sitting up, Amber curled her knees back and chewed on her lower lip as she considered Joe. Temptation tore her in half as she thought about the man in front of her. He was the kind of guy girls took chances on. "She thinks marriage is an institution designed to imprison a woman and reduce her to a possession. She burned her bra and kicked my father out of the house because he asked her to marry him. If I called up and told her I was getting married, she just might disown me. She thinks marriage forces a woman to live in monogamy against her natural need to find the strongest male."

"I am the strongest male, baby." Joe's eyes dropped to her nipples and the disobedient flesh rose into points for him. Satisfaction crossed his face before he looked back at her face. Relief crashed into Amber as she watched Joe take in every taboo idea she'd just voiced without flinching.

"So I guess that line about her cursing her cheating boyfriend was just clever female thinking on your part?"

"You heard that?" Amber hadn't really thought too much about what Joe and his men had overheard, she'd just been grateful they had shown up.

"It sounded almost too wild not to be true."

"Well, you might not want to know what parts were based on fact. My mom lives an open lifestyle." Amber tried to swallow as Joe flung his shirt aside. The way the man's chest made her feel was downright wrong. Normal thought patterns dissipated into a cloud of sexual fantasy.

"Which part—the voodoo or the curse on you? And just why are you so worried about it? Your mom isn't the one I'm interested in getting naked with."

"My mom isn't happy about some of my personal religious choices." Amber watched his face to see what effect that tidbit had.

"She'll have to learn to be open-minded and accept me the way I am too." Joe dropped his jeans and Amber felt her retort die on her lips. He moved towards the bed in a stunning display of male power. The mattress bounced as he dropped onto it and pushed her back.

"I did not agree to sleep with you again." Her body had but Amber had to hold her lips in a tight line because she was having just a little too much fun baiting Joe. She did want to sleep with him. Excitement raced through her body but there was also an edge of fun to it. She could play with Joe and it made the sex so much more intimate.

His fingers brushed one nipple and she groaned. Pleasure zipped down her body and caused her belly to twist into a knot. He lifted his dark eyes to stare into her as he moved those fingers back across her nipple once more.

"Well, honey, if you want to leave…" His hand cupped her breast. "Knowing I'm laying here dreaming about you…" His lips landed on hers and thought melted into the lava flowing through her body. He thrust his tongue into her mouth as he took his time with the kiss. It was deep and warm and tasted completely male.

Amber lifted her hands and laid them on the shoulders that her eyes couldn't stay away from. She smoothed her fingertips along the ridges of hard muscle and let her tongue go searching for his. Joe's hands covered her breasts as he gently squeezed them and rolled the nipples between his fingers. Hunger gnawed at her as he pressed one knee between her thighs.

His cock was raging once again and Joe didn't bother to wonder why. He wanted her and only her. The desire twisted around his brain, taking over every thought process he owned. The way she tasted made him edgy, the little mutters of pleasure coming from her lips bred possessiveness. Their topic of conversation should have turned him cold, instead all he thought about was getting back into the hot little passage that he could smell as he spread her thighs.

"How are you feeling now, Amber?"

Joe's eyes were dark as they cut into hers. Male pride stared back at her as he nodded his head and dipped his mouth towards her breasts. Amber arched her back from sheer need as his lips closed around one beaded nipple. Pleasure snaked down her spine until it hit her passage. Fluid seeped down to the knee touching her sex as his mouth lingered over her breast. A whimper came from her lips as she twisted and yearned for more than the pressure of his knee. Joe wouldn't give it to her while his pride smarted. Her temper didn't arrive to help her any. Instead all she felt was the burning pull of complete intimacy.

"I can't think when you touch me. All I want is you. There has to be something wrong with me."

His head rose above hers and those eyes cut into hers once again. "Maybe, maybe not. Every time I get a whiff of your skin, I get a little crazy too." His hand traveled down her torso and through the curls on the top of her sex. "All I think about is discovering whether or not you're wet for me." One finger parted her folds and slipped into the heavy fluid seeping from her passage. His mouth hardened as her hips tipped up for that finger. "And then when I can smell your body, I go insane with the need to fuck you."

Joe thrust his finger into her passage and watched her eyes dilate with pleasure. Her hips lifted for the penetration as a little moan escaped her lips. His cock jerked as he pulled his finger back and rubbed it along her slit until he found the little bud at the top of her folds. Her juices coated his hand as he rubbed the little bundle of nerves and listened to her whimper with need.

"Have you decided where you want to sleep yet, Amber? I don't mind waiting for a while if you want to keep thinking."

His finger froze and his hip held her pelvis solidly on the surface of the bed. She was on the edge of release but Joe denied her the friction she craved. His eyes cut into hers as he refused to let her linger in half decisions. He wouldn't give her sex without commitment.

"I'm sleeping here." He rolled over and she almost screamed. But his hands caught her body and took her with him. One hand gripped each hip as he lifted her above him. His back was on the mattress as Amber rose above him. Her knees landed on either side of his lean hips as his hands held her right above his cock. Joe lifted her until she was poised over his cock. He gently lowered her until the head of his cock nudged the folds of her body and slipped into her passage.

"Show me how you like it, honey." His eyes were cut with harsh victory as her body weight helped impale her on his cock. His hand gripped her hips to steady her but didn't raise her off his cock. "Ride me."

Amber shivered at the raw face of her partner. His eyes were almost savage as she used her thighs to rise off his length and then push back onto him. His fingers cut into her hips as his hips thrust up from the surface of the bed but she controlled the rate of penetration. The control was empowering. She lifted her body and eased it slowly back onto his cock. His teeth bared but he didn't order her to change the pace.

"That's it, baby, take me."

Amber couldn't stop her body from doing just that. She needed the motion as badly as he did. She rose and fell as her body jerked with pleasure. Joe's hands held her steady as she moved faster. His eyes fastened onto her breasts as she moved. The heat burning from his eyes made her bolder. Lifting her arms she cupped her own breasts and fingered the tight nipples.

Joe bucked under her but his eyes were glued to her fingers as they rolled and pinched her nipples. One of his hands suddenly moved across her belly to the top of her sex. His eyes lifted to lock with hers. "Don't stop." This time his voice was thick with demand. His thumb found the nub at the top of her slit and rubbed the little button as she slid down his length.

A ragged moan erupted from her throat as she rose and he rubbed her once more on the downward plunge.

"Keep playing with those nipples, baby. I know you love it."

She didn't care! Her body was a solid stream of heat and pleasure. Everything revolved around the plunge of her hips. Joe bucked beneath her as she rode him, his eyes watching her breasts while he used that thumb to rub her clit.

"That's it, baby. Come!" Amber tumbled into climax as her hips plunged down onto his cock. Her body gripped his length and contracted around the hard cock.

"Yeah, baby, just like that."

Joe rose off the bed and rolled her over. His cock was still rock-hard as he pulled it out of her body. He piled three of the bed's pillows in the center of the mattress before he lifted her and laid her facedown over them. His hands adjusted her body so that her bottom was raised into the air by the pillows.

"Joe..."

"Shh, baby...you know I think your bottom is sexy as hell." One of his large hands smoothed over each cheek of her bottom as he moved behind her. "Fold your knees, baby."

Moving her legs, Amber took up her body weight with her thighs but her face flamed with a scarlet blush as she felt Joe rubbing her bottom again. She had never been on display before. She chewed on her lip as a little tingle of helplessness crossed her mind. With her head on the mattress she couldn't see what Joe was doing, only feel it and that left her anticipating with a nervous edge that had her nerve endings twitching.

"Tonight, we are playing command and compliance."

Amber surged off the bed but Joe was behind her and his ankles moved over hers as his hips thrust into her bottom keeping her thighs spread. He pushed her shoulders back down with one hand while his other one stroked her bottom again.

"Ah…someone needs to understand the rules of our new game." His hand slipped between her legs and rubbed her open slit. Pleasure shot into her belly as he found her clit and rubbed it before moving back along her open sex.

"I don't do bondage, Joe!"

"Have you tried it?" His voice was thick with anticipation and Amber couldn't hide the little pulse of excitement that raced through her. There was something about her current position that made her even hotter. His finger moved down her slit again as he leaned over her bent back. "Have you, baby?"

Right next to her ear his voice sounded as darkly excited as she felt. "No." His lips nipped her ear before trailing across her spine. He circled the opening to her body with his finger before rubbing her bottom again. A thin trail of fluid followed his hand and Amber shuddered as she realized how wet she was.

"Good." His body rose away from hers as he pulled his hand completely off her bottom. She was keenly aware of the lack of contact and her skin wailed at the loss.

"Ever been spanked?"

"No." Her voice sounded far too excited. Amber didn't recognize it. The nerve endings covering her bottom snapped to attention as Joe's words sparked an image of his hand returning to smack her upraised cheeks.

Instead the tip of his finger dipped into her pussy. Amber moaned as pleasure twisted the passage as it tried to contract around that single digit. All of her senses were alive with an intensity she'd never felt before. It was the idea of "what if" that made every touch so extreme. The head of his cock brushed against her thigh making her quiver with need.

"It excites you doesn't it, baby? The idea of what I might decide to do?" His finger moved deeper into her body and froze. "I could spank you or fuck you. Maybe both at the same time." His finger left and Amber whimpered as her passage felt empty. "I could sink my cock into that wet pussy and just sit there too."

"No."

A low rumble of male laughter hit her ears as he dipped his finger into her passage again. This time he trailed it up to her back opening. Leaning back over her body, he licked her ear once again. "Ever had a man back here?"

The idea was so forbidden, Amber just shook her head. But she couldn't stop the little zings of pleasure that came from that finger as it circled and spread her own lubrication over her back entrance. Joe sat back up and the skin on her back felt chilled without his body.

He spanked her. One blow hit her right cheek and stayed there as the sting traveled through her body. The hand left and Amber felt every nerve ending twist with excitement as she waited for the next blow to land.

It had to be one of the most exciting moments she'd ever endured. Amber didn't care about right or wrong. Joe spanked her left cheek and her passage contracted with the blow. The cries coming out of her mouth didn't matter either. The only thing that mattered was the way Joe had of making her body transform into a mass of receptors that functioned only for pleasure.

"You like that, baby, don't you?"

Amber shook her head as another slap landed on her raised bottom. "Not good enough, Amber. Tell me, baby."

"Yes! Yes, I like it." His hand delivered two more blows before he leaned over her back again.

"You like being spanked?"

Amber whimpered as her body began to twist and contort with need. Joe cupped a breast as he covered her back and pinched the nipple with his fingers. Her bottom was on fire and her passage screamed for the hard cock teasing her thigh. "Joe, please!"

"Easy, baby, I'll take care of you." He left her back and thrust into her body in one smooth motion. Amber cried as she was stretched around his length. The walls of her passage clenched as he pulled out and slammed back into her.

"Tell me how you want it, Amber." His voice was tight with his own need. Amber opened her eyes to see her fingers fisted into the bedding as she lifted her bottom for his next thrust.

"Hard… Oh, Joe…spank me too!"

He growled through his teeth and it made her scream. Amber pushed her bottom towards him as his hand landed on her with a hard slap. His cock rammed into her body as he slapped her bottom again. All the sensation coursed into her womb as his other hand reached around her hip to the top of her slit and the little nub sitting there. She burst into climax the second he touched her clit. The pleasure broke around the hard thrust of his cock as one more spank completed her rapture.

Joe growled as she felt the hot splash of seed shoot into her. His hands curled around her hips as he pulled her back onto his cock. Her body pitched as she struggled to pull air into her lungs. Joe's hands smoothed over her bottom as his hips made little thrusting motions and his cock twitched inside her passage.

The bed rocked as Joe rolled over and lifted her off the pillows. His hand sent them flying off the bed as he pulled her against his body. His hands smoothed over her curves as he let their legs tangle.

Amber fell asleep in his embrace. Joe indulged himself with rubbing her bottom before pulling a blanket over her cooling skin. Their legs tangled as he adjusted her body around his. His cock still twitched as the scent of her climax hit his nose. He could spend all night inside her body and not get enough. She was a potent combination of spunk and sex appeal that went straight to his head. It really didn't matter why.

What mattered to him was the echo of her words that said she was sleeping in his bed. The rest of it could go hang itself.

Chapter Eleven

"This is Idaho, you'll love it there."

Flamingo didn't look at the computer screen. Instead the tortoise lowered his head to investigate Amber's toes.

"I am going to move us there but don't worry about the snow, I'll get you a nice garage to live in during the winter."

Snip smothered a laugh from the hallway and Amber glared at the SEAL.

"Just as soon as this stupid trial is over, Flamingo, we are headed to Idaho!"

The tortoise tried to eat her toes in response. Amber yelped and jumped out of her chair. More choking sounds came from the hallway as she hopped towards the kitchen.

"But first I'll make your salad."

"Are you making lunch for me?"

Amber jumped at the voice. She knew there was a wide set of shoulders in the doorway but had assumed it was Snip or one of the other SEALs. She wasn't quite ready to face Joe yet. He'd been thankfully absent when she woke up this morning. Doing that in his bed certainly didn't help her ignore the collapse of her self-determination the night before but it was easier to bear when she wasn't facing those dark eyes.

"Amber, hon, that eggplant looks like it has seen better days. I can get you some fresh produce."

"Flamingo isn't picky about his salad. In fact, he's rather good at recycling old produce. I asked for the old stuff because feeding Flamingo can get costly. The grocer sometimes sells his trimmings for pet food."

"Yeah?" Joe looked at the large reptile as it sniffed at the air. Amber was chopping up a mountain of vegetables and had a stack of greens on the counter. She scraped the whole mess into a bowl and stacked the bundles of greens on top.

Amber pushed the back door open with her hip and balanced her mound of tortoise chow in her arms. Joe suddenly found the sight charming. It was almost like the house lit up as she moved around it doing something as common as kitchen duty.

The wind howled in the open door. Dirt and dry leaves tumbled across the floor before Amber hurried back inside as she rubbed her arms.

His lips turned into a frown as he realized he'd been looking forward to coming home tonight. Anticipating the fact that Amber would be here, in his house, when he got there. The emotion went beyond sex. What he was looking forward to was Amber, the sexy and the spunky woman who seemed to have merged into his life in the last week.

"I've got some good news for you."

Amber was almost afraid to discover just what Joe had on his mind. His face was a guarded mask that didn't give her even a tiny hint. Instead his eyes were intensely sharp as they scrutinized her.

"The judge will see you tomorrow morning. That should put an end to any problems from Dantrolp. It's a official deposition to keep any further attempts on your life from happening."

Amber waited for relief to cross her mind. Instead she felt like her dream vacation was about to end. The last of the bees were gone and the little guesthouse would be perfectly safe for her to move back into.

She could not do it. There was no way she could live there. Amber refused to name the reason why but she just knew that being around Joe and not touching him was going to be impossible to endure.

The wind picked up and sent some tree branches against the kitchen window. Joe turned his head to consider the plane of glass. "Boy, it's really picking up out there." Dark rain clouds were being shoved together by the gusts of wind. The swollen purple mass promised a Texas-size thunderstorm within an hour.

The lights flickered as the wind whistled under the door. There was an odd creaking sound from the roof a second before the sliding glass door shattered. Half an oak tree came through it as the wind whipped the broken tree around like a leaf. The power died as broken glass scattered on the kitchen floor.

"Amber?" Heavy footfalls hit his ears as his men converged on the kitchen. "Clear!" Joe yelled the command as he watched his SEALs enter the scene, muzzle-first.

Cussing filled the kitchen as they tried to pull the branch away from the wall. One slim hand was the only sign of Amber as Joe brutally lifted the mass of broken wood off her.

"Amber?" Joe gently reached for her face to brush the hair back from it. She was slumped onto the tile floor like a marionette whose strings were cut. Snip knelt on a pile of broken glass and wood chips as he scanned her body for injury. Blood seeped from a cut on her hair as Joe smoothed the mess of tangled red hair and wood bark away from her eyes.

"Flamingo, Mama wants to sleep. I'll feed you later." Amber brushed his hand aside and rubbed her forehead. She didn't open her eyes but her forehead creased with pain as she rubbed it once more.

"Amber? Wake up, honey."

"Hmm?" Amber tried to think but it hurt too much. She rubbed at the persistent pain before pushing Flamingo away again. "You are an animal with a one-track mind. Just a walking stomach."

Her slurred words still made Joe grin like an idiot. Her eyelashes fluttered as she opened them and stared at him. "Hi, honey." Joe felt his relief drain away as she couldn't seem to focus her eyes on him. Instead she looked past him as she rubbed her head once more. Her legs moved as she tried to push herself off the floor.

"Whoa. Stay right there, Amber."

She hissed at him but Joe firmly pressed her to the kitchen floor. "Let me up before Flamingo sits on me."

Snip cussed and snickered at the same time. Flamingo had walked right in through the shattered door and was bearing down on his owner. Snip made a grab for the determined reptile and the giant tortoise dragged the man forward.

"You are one big boy, all right!" Snip got his feet under him and began to pull the tortoise away from Amber. The heels of his boots skidded on the tile as he dug in to hold back her pet. Joe looked back to see her eyes focused on his and a harassed look on her face.

"Told you to let me up. Flamingo goes wherever he wants to go." There were a few grunts from Snip as his boots slipped on the floor while he wrestled with the animal.

Amber slowly sat up and watched the world tilt as she did it. She blinked her eyes as she forced them to come back into focus. Snip was telling Flamingo to go on a diet as the SEAL half-dragged her unhappy pet into the yard. A heavy gust of wind whipped into the kitchen carrying the scent of rain.

"He doesn't like rain."

Joe let out a whistle that Snip immediately responded to. "Frank doesn't like rain. Put him in the garage."

"Have you tried moving this animal, sir?"

"Use a piece of cantaloupe."

"For what?" Amber got to her feet and Snip propped his hands on his hips as he glared at her.

"Flamingo will follow a piece of cantaloupe almost anywhere."

A smile brightened the SEAL's face before he picked up a freshly cut slice of melon from the pile of food that Amber had left for her pet. Flamingo lifted his nose and began following the offered treat.

A blanket suddenly wrapped around her shoulders before Joe picked her up and carried her through the destroyed kitchen. Every step he took sent a ripple of pain through her skull.

"Joe, where are we going?"

"To a hospital."

"I don't need a doctor. It's just a knock on the head." Amber was about to add that it happened rather regularly but decided Joe just might admit her to the psych ward if she made any comments about curses at the moment.

She landed in the front seat of his truck in response. His eyes surveyed her face with critical movement before he buckled the seat belt for her.

It was so tempting to just lean on him. When fate hiccupped, it was always her and Flamingo against the forces of nature. Joe and his strength shimmered like a mirage as her head ached and her scalp itched. Reaching for the one thing she could change, Amber sent her finger through her hair to the annoying tingle.

Her fingers found a wet mat instead. Pain was instant as she touched the injury and Joe pulled her hand away the second he slid in beside her. Amber stared at the bright red blood covering her fingers.

"On the other hand, I shouldn't let all those health care benefits go to waste."

"Amber honey, you are turning my hair grey." She smiled at him. Joe couldn't stop the little chuckle that rumbled out of his chest. Who else could manage to get knocked flat by a tree branch while standing in a kitchen? Just his Little Red.

"You need a keeper." And Joe was looking at the position more and more as the days went by. "And we need to have a talk about just what part of your mom cursing you was true. I know a good preacher and I'm open to negotiation with the woman. But I'm going to make her understand a thing or two about laying down bad karma on my woman."

"You won't like the answer you get, Joe."

He slid her a sidelong glance as the truck covered the road in a smooth hum. "It really doesn't matter to me beyond her accepting you for what you are. A parent should always be happy to see their kids spread their wings and fly. Your mom doesn't have to like your life decisions but she can aim her negative energy someplace else. It's that simple to me."

His face told her the subject was closed. Amber almost giggled and handed him her cell phone. Her mom wouldn't find Joe as simple to bend as some of the other guys she'd dated. Amber liked that fact. She liked it a whole lot as she considered the rather relaxed attitude Joe had about a lot of things. She liked him far too much as his words set aside her fears.

It was way too late to move to Idaho.

* * * * *

"You are going to be the death of me," Joe muttered under his breath as Amber gave him a sleepy smile. She wiggled her bottom against him as she muttered in her sleep. Joe didn't move away from her body. Tucking her into his bed had seemed vitally important to him. His arms were wrapped around her sleeping form as he continued to just absorb her presence in his bed.

It had been intensely enjoyable to put her into his bed once he got her home from the emergency room. His cock burned as that sassy seat pressed against it. Joe enjoyed the burn of arousal as he resigned himself to going to sleep hungry. Well, going to bed. Sleep was miles away but he was staying right next to Amber. Why didn't matter, in fact he didn't care. Sometimes when you found something that made you happy, a man needed to be smart enough to run with it.

Amber was burning alive. She couldn't sleep. Instead something nagged her to wake up completely. Her body was completely happy and it seemed to promise her even better bliss if she would just wake up.

Her eyelids lifted to show her a dark room. It wasn't completely pitch-black. Light came from the bathroom where Joe liked to keep one of the closet lights on. That was just another one of the little details that defined the kind of harsher man that he was. Joe didn't leave anything to chance. He was always thinking about defense and making certain he had angles covered. His gun had been tucked in between the mattress and the headboard when she'd woken up that morning and she was positive the black weapon was there right now.

"Go back to sleep, honey." A warm hand smoothed her eyes closed but her brain shook off any hint of slumber as her ears recognized the husky note in Joe's voice. Hunger coated the dark rich male tone and her body erupted in response. It was that simple. Joe's hard body was pressed along her back and all she could do was smell how incredibly male his skin was.

Her hips gave a wiggle without her conscious thought. The cheeks of her bottom seemed determined to show her exactly how hard his cock was. Heat flowed down her passage as that thick rod pressed into her bottom.

Joe clamped a hand onto her hip as sweat beaded on his forehead. He drew a harsh breath into his lungs and reminded himself that he'd just brought her home from the emergency room. His goddamn cock was just going to have to wait!

"Go to sleep, baby." Her body shivered as he caught the unmistakable scent of her hot arousal. Joe couldn't ever remember knowing what any other woman smelled like but he knew Amber's scent. His nostrils flared as his cock throbbed with the need to bury itself in her body. Pump his seed into the dark center of her womb and hold her while every last drop of his cum was emptied into this woman.

"Make me."

"Amber…the doctor said rest."

She giggled before turning her head and looking over her shoulder at him. "All right, we won't do the bent over the pillows thing tonight. You'll just have to choose a different position." His eyes narrowed at her but Amber didn't care, his breath was still rasping in through his gritted teeth. Joe wasn't mad, he was hungry and she suddenly clearly understood the difference. She wasn't mad about him putting her into his bed either. Sure, there were plenty of emotions attached to the idea of sleeping with the man but she wasn't angry about it.

Passion appeared to bind them together in some ritual of burning need. Letting down your guard wasn't something either of them did gracefully but right then it didn't matter nearly as much as the hard cock pressing against her bottom.

Joe grunted at her with stubborn male pride. Amber muttered under her breath at the man's low opinion of her physical endurance.

"Amber, don't push, honey. That seat of yours drives me insane. I'd love to get inside you but I sure as hell won't be gentle about it, so go to sleep."

"Fine, then I am going to sleep in the guestroom, because I can't sleep next to you and not get...ideas. I don't like this game," Amber announced to her stubborn bed partner.

"We are not playing a game, Amber. You are resting."

Joe was agitated and Amber giggled over the cause. Who might have guessed that she could find the calm to deal with a huge predator of a man like Joe when he was feeling ornery?

"You are trying to play Simon Says and I broke the rules the last time you tried to get me to face off with you."

"If I was going to say something I thought you would do without question, you can bet it would be a whole lot more than sleep."

"Bring it on, big boy." Amber wiggled against his cock again and smiled as Joe's breath hissed through his teeth. His fingers dug into her hips but there was still a small thrust from his that pressed their lower bodies together. "That's much better."

Amber almost purred the words and Joe felt his sanity crumbling. His nostrils caught the warm scent of arousal and his fingers changed their hold on her hips. Now he moved her into alignment with his body. Her bottom lifted for him as he nuzzled the warm skin of her neck.

"I'm not that fragile, Joe. It's just a few stitches. If you insist on putting me to bed every time I get a little bruised, I'm going to spend half my life in bed."

"Now I like the sound of that idea." Joe nipped the spot where her shoulder and neck met as she purred once again. His hands gently cupped her breasts before slipping towards her hips again. She was right and Joe enjoyed discovering he was wrong for once. Amber wasn't weak.

She took things in stride, it was one of the things that made her so appealing to him.

"Well, I don't. I took care of myself just fine without you."

His eyes darkened as his lips thinned into a tight line. Joe smoothed a warm hand over each of her breasts before he caught her chin and captured her mouth with his. His kiss was hard and demanding. He pushed into her mouth and stroked her tongue with his. Desire snaked towards her belly as he thrust that tongue deeply into her before pulling his lips away.

"Amber, you never took care of what I do to you. But I think I might just enjoy your appetite, baby." His head disappeared over her shoulder again as he clamped her body to his.

Amber listened to the little sounds coming through her lips like they belonged to a stranger. Joe slid one firm hand over her belly to the top of her mons. She quivered as she anticipated him slipping that hand under her nightgown and finding the little bundle of nerves at the top of her cleft. Her skin tightened as she felt the skin on skin contact as his fingers lifted the thin cotton fabric and found her bare thigh.

"Slow and easy, baby. I wouldn't want to put you to bed hungry."

His knee slipped between her thighs and her folds opened for that hand. His fingers gently parted the soft curls on her mons before slipping into her slit.

Joe gritted his teeth as he felt the slick flesh waiting for him. It was a delicious torture to slip his finger down the length of her sex to the opening of her passage and back up to the little nub at the top of her slit. Feeling how wet she was drove him to the edge of reason as he moved his finger back to the opening of her passage. Her bottom wiggled as she whimpered and Joe gently rubbed around the opening.

"Yeah honey, we are going to take a whole lot of time tonight."

Amber felt her belly tighten almost unbearably with tension. She wasn't sure if it was excitement or fear but it combined into a heat that left her panting. His finger teased her. One firm tip moved through her folds. It was a slow journey that had the skin in its path begging for contact long before he touched it. The opening of her passage craved its turn to be stroked as she noticed how empty her body felt. The hard length of his cock burned against her bottom taunting her with its thick width.

"I'm not going to fuck you tonight, Amber." Joe whispered his words next to her ear. She trembled as she listened to his hard voice. The predator was awake and demanding to be in control of their intimacy. He wanted control and her body seemed desperate to yield it. "I'm going to screw you, baby, real slow and deep."

Amber felt heat engulf her body as his words repeated in her brain. She should have been angry. There should have been some protest from her pride but all she found was the growing hunger to submit to his demand. It would test his control and there was an almost primal surge of excitement attached to that idea.

"If you think you can. I'd like to see you try."

He growled in her ear. Amber was half certain he knew what kind of primitive sound he made and did it on purpose for her to hear. That mixture of fear and excitement curled into her womb as she felt her hips lifting towards him.

His knee bent between her thighs and lifted her leg as he rolled slightly back. His other leg trapped her right leg to the surface of the bed. Joe spread her thighs wide as his finger circled the opening to her passage. His legs twisted with her and trapped her spread open for his amusement.

"You still so sure, baby?" His teeth nipped the column of her neck before biting a path towards her shoulder. Her hips twitched towards his finger as her passage begged for penetration but Joe tightened his thighs and rubbed his digit back towards her clit.

Amber cried out as he touched her little bud. The pleasure was so acute she couldn't contain the sound. Joe pressed and rubbed over the bundle of nerves as he held her spread open for his touch.

"I can smell you… Did you know that, Amber? Right now, the scent of your body is driving me nearly mad. All I can think about is how wet you are." His finger pressed and held as she shivered on the edge of climax. "But you could get wetter, with the right stimulation."

Suddenly he was gone. Amber fell onto the bed and groaned. The sound came from her womb as it begged for the climax that had teased it. Instead she searched the dark room for the shadow that shifted and moved back to her side.

Joe pushed her thighs apart with his shoulders as he came back to the bed. Amber fell back as she shivered with anticipation once again. His voice was so menacing, it promised her complete mastery, and maybe there was a secret part of her that craved to be bent into submission.

A small buzz hit her ears as Joe spread her thighs even wider. His face lowered over her spread sex as he leveled a wicked grin at her. He penetrated her body with something that vibrated. Just slightly thicker than one of his fingers, he pushed the device into her wet passage.

"Joe!"

"Shhh…baby, you tossed down the gauntlet. Now, I'm going to make you scream."

Her eyes went wide and round and Joe chuckled. He wanted to make her scream, all right. There was something pulsing through his brain that demanded he take her body to a level of pleasure that would make her scream. Maybe it was ego but Joe caught the scent of her body as he adjusted the little vibrator inside her before spreading the folds of her sex apart to bare her little clit. He blew on the little bud first and her hips jerked. Her flesh glistened as he leaned forward to gently lick her.

"Joe!"

He chuckled and applied his tongue over her again. Amber felt her spine arch as pleasure shot up from the contact. The little vibrator hummed away inside her as Joe used only his tongue to drive her insane. She was balanced on the edge of climax but he kept her there as the tip of his tongue circled and rubbed her clit.

"I always make sure I have the right equipment for every mission too, baby. I picked up a few toys for us to play with today."

Her little whimper excited him. Joe caught her clit with his lips and sucked on the little center of pleasure. Her hips bucked as he let her body climax. His cock was aching but he enjoyed the hard bite of it as he listened to

Amber sob. Satisfaction pumped through his brain as he continued to suck and rub her clit.

She never came down from the peak. Amber tried to catch her breath but her lungs couldn't keep up with her heart rate. Joe still had her bud between his lips as his fingers gently rubbed the opening to her passage. He grasped the little vibrator as his tongue resumed licking across her clit. Pleasure ripped through her as he gently worked the little sex toy in and out of her body. The walls of her passage begged for the penetration the second it slid out of her. Thoughts refused to form in her brain. Instead everything centered under his tongue as he licked and sucked in time with the penetration of the vibrator. Need became almost cruel as it twisted and bit into her body. Climax refused to relieve the ache as Joe held her down for more of the stimulation.

"Joe, please!"

He didn't laugh at her plea. Instead his head rose to aim his eyes at her face. Deep male satisfaction glittered from his eyes as he pushed the vibrator into her passage while he watched her.

"Are we done playing, baby?"

"Yes!"

"Roll over and pull your knees under you."

There was a part of him that enjoyed watching her obey. Joe put his feet onto the floor and stood up as she flipped onto her stomach and scooted back until she was on her haunches. He reached for her hips and pulled her to the edge of the bed.

"That's it, baby."

The hard thrust of his cock against her leg drove her insane. Amber whimpered as she pushed her body towards Joe. She needed to be filled and her body screamed for the hard thrust of his. The little vibrator buzzed away inside her as Joe stroked her bottom.

"I bought you a plug today."

She reared off the bed but Joe pushed her right back down. His hand smacked her bottom as she gasped, the spanking combined with the vibration making her pant as a contraction of pleasure crossed her belly.

"A small plug that will make your pussy even tighter when I screw you." He slapped the opposite side of her bottom making pleasure shoot through her again.

He reached for the bedside table and pulled the drawer open. His hand brought two items out of it before he spanked her bottom once again. All the while the vibrator continued its function. Her body was balanced on the edge of climax but never allowed to dive into it.

Joe's fingers gently retrieved the little sex toy and silenced it. The silver vibrator landed on the bed next to her as he fingered her back entrance. There was the smooth touch of some kind of lubrication before one finger pressed against her for entrance.

"Joe, that isn't my idea of a good time!"

His finger pressed and entered her body, making her gasp. "You said the same thing about being spanked, honey." Her face flushed but her mind instantly demanded she let Joe try his plug on her. The spanking had made her scream. His cock already filled her completely, she shuddered as she contemplated how much tighter she'd be with a plug in.

"Yeah, baby, you're thinking about how good it might be, aren't you?" His finger moved around the tight muscle as he spread more lubricant over her bottom. The first touch of the plug made her nervous. It had always been taboo in her mind but trust held her still as it pressed into her bottom.

Trust in Joe, the man would kill for her and she knew without doubt he wouldn't injure her.

"Yeah, baby, you know I can handle you, don't you?" Amber whimpered as the plug pressed into her bottom. Sensation so sharp hit her body, she shivered as she felt it lodge completely inside her. Joe's fingers traced her slit until they found her clit once again. Pleasure shot into her womb as she cried out.

"Turn over." His voice made her purr. It was hard and cut with tension, betraying his level of need. Amber rolled onto her back and let her eyes trace the naked feast his body presented. Moonlight bathed his bare body and flowed over each ridge and muscle. Her eyes lingered over the hard erection stabbing towards her as Joe reached for her thighs and pulled her to the edge of the bed.

His body stepped between her legs making her spread even further apart for him. The head of his cock probed her as she tried to move up towards the penetration she craved. His hands gripped her hips and forced her to stay in place.

"Don't move, Amber." His voice was rough and dark. Amber shivered at the pure dominance being demanded but her body refused to care how it got what it craved. Only that the hard cock teasing her passage, penetrated and filled the yearning space.

"I told you, baby. Tonight, it will be slow and deep." He thrust into her body with his words. The hard length of his cock stretched her passage as he groaned. The plug made his penetration even tighter and the pleasure acute.

His hands smoothed over her hips before gripping them as he pulled his cock out of her body. Amber whimpered as she was once again empty. Joe paused with just the tip of his cock inside her before he slowly pushed it back into her.

"I could spend an hour just like this." He was deep inside her body as his words hit her almost like a threat. Amber craved more friction but he held her stretched on his length before slowly pulling his cock from her again.

Pleasure twisted with need as the slow thrusting allowed her to linger in each and every second like it was an eternity. This time there wasn't the white-hot eruption of pleasure. Instead Amber felt like she was burning alive. His hands smoothed over her bottom before he thrust back into her passage.

She was so damn sexy. Joe clenched his teeth as he thrust over and over into her body. He tightened his control and refused the screaming need to rut on her like a beast. His cock throbbed and he enjoyed the hard edge of the sensation. Her body was soaking wet as he thrust and withdrew, never increasing the pace. Instead he listened to his heartbeat pound past his ears as he forced them both to endure the deep penetration and that full moment that he lingered deep inside her.

Amber's cries became desperate. Joe opened his eyes as he drew his next thrust along her clit.

"Are you ready, baby?"

"Oh, God yes!"

His finger rubbed over her clit and Amber shook as pleasure twisted every nerve ending she had. Joe thrust into her as his finger rubbed and her cry hit the darkness. It ripped from her throat as pleasure ripped into her womb and her passage clutched at his hard cock. Joe's harsh grunt told her his control was at its limit. One hard thrust and his seed splashed into her body. Their cries were sounds of primitive satisfaction. It bounced off the walls of the room, filling their ears to the point where Amber couldn't separate anything. Pleasure twisted her like a sheet left on a drying line and her body gripped Joe's cock, desperate to hold onto the essence of life.

Harsh…primitive and completely mind-blowing. Joe watched her in the dark with glittering eyes before he pulled the little plug from her bottom. He ripped a pillowcase off a pillow and cleaned her body before lifting her and placing her under the covers.

He melted into the dark bathroom as Amber listened to the sound of running water. Sleep clouded her thoughts so she didn't try to think anymore. Her body hummed with contentment as her limbs relaxed.

The bed bounced as Joe rolled onto it. His arms took her with him as he rolled onto his back and pressed her head to his chest. His heart pounded beneath the hard muscle and Amber sighed. She was surrounded by the scent of him, encased in the strength that made her body so content in his embrace. Nothing else mattered but the harmony their bodies seemed to produce together.

"Joe? I think I like playing games with you."

"More than you like Idaho?"

She made a little hum of amusement before nuzzling against his chest once more. "Maybe."

That one little word lifted the corners of his mouth until he was grinning like a schoolkid. Joe stroked the side of her face as she slept and grinned some more. Sometimes you just went with an emotion and didn't question why it showed up.

Chapter Twelve

It was amazing how something so important could happen so quickly. Amber looked at the Area Judge and waited for him to cross-examine her. Instead he laced his fingers together and considered her rather meager answers to his questions.

Amber wasn't sure what she had expected but such a calm ending to her week of premium security hadn't been it. The judge had seen her in his chambers due to her recent connection with a tree. Amber doubted the stitches in her scalp were the real reason. The Texas Governor was listening on speakerphone and Joe's Navy team had the doors sealed.

"Thank you, Ms. Talisman. I appreciate you doing your duty and testifying."

She waited for relief to show up. Instead she almost felt like crying. The judge stood up and offered her his hand to shake. The ordeal wasn't truly over but now that she'd given her testimony there was no reason to kill her any longer. The court recorder could just read her words to a jury. That meant she was free to go home.

The idea of her new satin and lace bed in the cottage made her throat choke up.

Oh Lord, Amber!

She could just chew up her stubborn pride and tell Joe she wanted to stay. That would require a whole lot of jaw work but it wasn't impossible. Men and women negotiated relationships all the time.

Fear was an emotion very similar to mold. Just as soon as you thought you had killed it, the stubborn stuff grew back. The truth was she was downright scared of being rejected. Her crazy life had never really bothered her. Of course she could face the fact that Joe might not be interested in anything more than sex.

Her thoughts kept her company on the way home. Amber grinned at the house as Joe drove into the drive. Flamingo was wandering around the side yard as he grazed on the grass.

Joe leaned against his truck to watch Amber. She'd leapt out of his vehicle the second he hit the brakes and was talking to her pet. Tension knotted his neck muscles as he considered how confident she really was on her own. There was a part of him that would have loved to see some kind of attachment to him linger in her eyes.

A little grin crossed his face as Amber bent over and showed off her bottom to him. Naw, he liked his Little Red exactly the way she was.

Joe's phone rang and she listened to the deep sound of his voice as he answered it. Moving towards the house, Amber went towards her own job. At least for the moment, she had things to fill up her brain with. Tonight, she'd just have to think about her move to Idaho.

Her things were still in the master bedroom. It was really silly to feel odd about going into Joe's room but Amber felt her stomach give a little flop in her belly as she approached the doorway.

Her jaw dropped as she took in the room. Her new satin and lace comforter was covering the bed. Joe's ultra-male flannel sheets were gone too, and the pale green satin ones she'd bought covered the mattress.

"I used to think my Navy pals were cracked to put up with a wife who bought satin bed coverings." Joe's hand smoothed down her back as he appeared silently next to her. It was little things like that that reminded her of his deadly abilities. There was an everyday Joe that was comfortable and loose, but hidden inside him was something much less...tame.

That excited her. Amber licked her lower lip as she thought about the raw aggression he sometimes let emerge. The fact that she never knew when to expect that harder edge made it so much more exciting. She looked at the bedding and shivered. Joe had planned ahead of her once again. Not only was the satin on his bed, one of his SEAL buddies had done the job.

"I thought you said my bedding needed a warning sign."

"It still does." His hand gave a controlled push that sent her into the bedroom. Joe stood in the doorway as Amber turned to look at the raw hunger blazing from his face. She licked her lower lip again and his eyes homed in on the little motion.

"Your bed needs a huge warning posted above it to any other man who even thinks about sniffing around it."

His eyes darkened as Amber let her eyes drop to the crotch of his pants. She wanted him to see her doing that. There was a naughty little desire racing through her brain to push him. Her body responded so intensely to his it was almost vital that she wield the same power over Joe.

"I love the way you look at me, baby." Joe walked to the bedside table and placed his gun on it. His eyes traveled over her body and lingered on her breasts. "Undress for me, Amber."

Her lips twitched up into a little grin as Amber fingered the top button on her top. Joe's eyes were devoted to her tiny motions as she pushed the little piece of plastic through its hole. She ran her hand down to the next button and popped it open. Confidence surged through her as she watched Joe's skin draw taut across his cheekbones. Last night he'd stopped just short of overwhelming her. The devotion radiating from his face restored the balance in their relationship.

It was her turn to stimulate.

Amber turned around as she opened the last button. She let the blouse hang open as she looked over her shoulder at Joe. Raising her hands she pulled her twin hair combs out and shook her head until her hair bounced onto her shoulders. Joe's lips tightened and gave her a glimpse of clenched teeth.

Rolling her shoulders, Amber let gravity take her blouse to the floor. She slipped her hands over her hips and Joe groaned.

"You could tease me to death, baby."

"You look mighty healthy to me, Josiah." Amber moved to the hook on her bra and opened it. "What's the matter? No stamina today?"

"You make me feel like a raw teenager, honey."

Amber hummed under her breath as Joe took a step towards her. "Oh no, you don't. A woman should never be rushed when she's undressing for a man."

Joe cussed under his breath but stood in place. He wanted to leap across the distance and strip her. Yank her skirt down her legs until he found warm skin and hot desire. But the promise in her eyes made him clamp his need into submission.

"I wouldn't dream of it."

"Hmmm…good boy." Amber dropped her bra and slid her hands down her bare sides to her skirt zipper. She gave a little wiggle of her hips as she pushed the zipper down and watched Joe's face as she did it. His eyes raked over her body like they owned it. Desire flamed up even further as she saw the raw animal in those eyes. He allowed her to taunt him and she felt excitement bleed from the idea that he could decide to stop being obedient at any second.

The skirt joined her clothing as she turned around. Only her thigh-high stockings and panties remained. They had lace edging that wrapped around each of her thighs and she was still in her high heels. A dangerous glint appeared in Joe's eyes as she showed off her almost nude body. Amber ran her tongue over her lower lip as she recognized that her turn was now very much…over.

Joe didn't make a sound as he approached. His motion was silent and practiced. His hands cupped her face as he gently licked her lips. He turned her face to fit their mouths together before pressing her for a deep kiss of ownership. Her hands rose to his shoulders as she delighted in running her fingers along his body.

"Now take my clothes off." He whispered the order next to her ear. Amber shivered at the hard promise in the male tones. Her hands instantly obeyed as they found the buttons on his shirt front and separated them from their holes. Crisp male hair sprang up through the opened sides of the garment. Amber unhooked the last button and slid her palms up the center of his body. The skin to skin contact made her shiver. Her nipples tightened into little pebbles as she separated her hands and ran them beneath the fabric to each of his shoulders. Amber pushed the shirt up and over those huge male shoulders and Joe moved his hands behind him so that the shirt fell to the floor.

His flat male nipples were as tightly beaded as her own. She stared at the little sign of his arousal and leaned towards one. Catching it between her lips, she let her tongue lick it as Joe hissed in response. The sound inflamed her courage making her move to his opposite nipple and lick it completely around before sucking its puckered tip into her mouth.

Her hands went south.

Amber purred around his nipple as she pulled his pants open. She trailed her lips over his abdomen as she sank to her knees and worked at the fly on his pants.

"I love the way you play with me, Little Red." His eyes aimed solid approval at her as his cock escaped the constriction of his pants. Amber slipped her fingers around his length before settling onto her knees.

"I think I could get used to daily matches myself."

Joe felt every muscle he owned freeze as she took his cock between her lips. Her red hair streamed down her shoulders as her mouth pulled more of his length into its hot center. Her little tongue licked around the head before finding the sensitive spot right underneath. She licked and rubbed as his hands gripped her hair. Pleasure shot down his body and back up to slam into his brain. Her fingers closed around the length left outside her mouth and she stroked it with a firm grip. The need to climax slammed into his skull but Joe pulled her away from his cock instead. She aimed amused eyes up to his as she leaned back to show him her coral nipples.

"I want to see you stretched out on that sea of satin and lace, baby. The idea has haunted me since I first saw it in your bedroom."

Amber pushed to her feet as her fingers lingered on his cock. Her body suddenly felt so empty. The walls of her passage begging for the hard thrust that would fill it with pleasure.

"I thought you didn't like it."

"Right up until I thought about you lying naked on it. Then I discovered a hidden craving for it to be on my bed."

Amber wanted to feed that craving. She backed away from his body and winked as she rolled right into the center of the bed. The satin was smooth beneath her back as she slipped her stocking-clad legs along each other and flipped her hair onto the comforter.

His eyes moved over her with complete possession. Amber stared at the stark bluntness of male ownership, and felt her heart melt. No gushing remark about how beautiful she was could have hit her harder. Joe tossed his jeans onto the floor as he dropped his eyes to her nipples.

The savage need to mate written on his face proved that she was the most amazing sight he had ever seen. It was an instinct centered somewhere in her brain that recognized that Joe wasn't just indulging his lust for her…he was mating with her.

Some people might call that making love. Amber felt it as complete, as the bed dipped when he placed a knee onto the mattress. Two hard fingers caught the edge of her panties and pulled. Amber lifted her hips as he tugged the little bit of satin down her body and tossed it onto the floor.

Joe was certain he was enchanted at the moment. Her body drew him to it with coral nipples and lush curves that whispered to his longings. Joe couldn't touch her in enough places at once. They rolled across the bed as they stroked and kissed with open need. His hips spread her thighs as she lifted her bottom for the hard thrust of his cock.

Her body was hot and wet, making him groan. Joe twisted his hands into her hair as his body pumped between her legs and pleasure exploded across them both. It was a timeless moment shared only by two people who were willing to let their separate personalities go. True intimacy wasn't something one person could touch, it took both partners holding onto only each other to reach its simmering folds. The night became an endless moment of pleasure as the world was forgotten and life simply ignored in the face of making love.

* * * * *

Joe kissed her lips as she woke up. Amber rubbed her eyes as sleep tempted her to return to it.

"I'll see you after work, honey."

Another warm kiss landed on her mouth as Joe stood up and left. Sunlight broke through the blinds as Amber watched his wide shoulders fill the doorway before he disappeared.

A little smile lifted her lips as she considered her day. There was nothing but normal, everyday things to do and not a cloak or dagger event in sight. No SEALs or drug dealers, just work and family and one giant opinionated reptile to deal with.

Now that was a good morning if ever there was one!

Chapter Thirteen

Joe called her before he left work. Amber slapped a hand over her face as a blush stained it. The beast didn't give her a chance to utter a single word. Instead his male voice filled her ear with a dark suggestion before the line snapped shut.

"I could just move to Idaho!"

Flamingo snorted and Amber glared at her pet. The tortoise began nuzzling the basketball and Amber jumped out of her sun chair. "Why do you have to be a male also?" Flamingo mounted the ball and Amber snorted.

Males! Men! It wasn't safe for a woman to breathe the same air! She stomped into the house but froze at the sight of Joe leaning against the doorway. He clipped his cell phone back onto his hip as he grinned at her.

"I thought I'd call a little closer to home, just in case the wait was unbearable."

"For who?"

Joe raised his eyebrow at her, making her stomp before she giggled again. Men! Well, actually, her problem wasn't with males—it was with one man! She couldn't stay mad at him. Even when he was being presumptuous, she found it too damn flattering!

Joe's eyes drifted over her face before they slipped down her body, igniting fire as they went. Her nipples beaded and her passage flooded. The heat doubled and tripled as he raised his eyes back to her face. The corners of his lips twitched up into a cocky grin as he laid his gun on the bedside table.

"Come over here, baby. I love the way you sweet-talk me."

A low chuckle came from his chest as he raised his hands to the top button on his shirt. Her mouth went dry as she watched the lean fingers push that little piece of plastic through its hole. The warm skin of his neck peeked at her as just a hint of chest hair curled between the edges of fabric. Another button separated and she felt her body leaning towards the warm male skin he was baring for her.

"Honey, when you tell me I make you want to toss aside every aspect of civilized behavior and just get naked, that's flattering."

"I don't remember offering to get naked."

Another button opened and she swallowed the lump in her throat. Naked sounded really good right then.

"Your eyes say it right now. So do those little nipples. God, I love those little coral tips."

Amber shivered but couldn't hold back her little naughty grin — she sure did love the fact that he liked her nipples! The thing the man did with his mouth made her hands lift and pull on her own shirt buttons. Getting naked with Joe seemed like the best idea she'd had all day!

"I want you to wear one thing to bed with me, honey."

Amber unhooked her bra and stopped as his words hit her. Joe's face was dead serious as he let the open shirt just hang. He stepped forward and caught her hand.

"Wear this, baby, and promise me you will never take it off."

Joe pushed the diamond engagement ring firmly up her finger before he let her see it. The little gem sparkled at her as she looked into the serious eyes of the man who still held her hand. He raised his eyebrow as one side of his mouth twitched up.

Amber stared at the little golden ring and felt tears prick her eyes. It felt so completely right on her hand. "But we just met...and isn't it supposed to take time to decide to ask a girl to marry you?"

"Of course, you're free to think about it." He bent and hefted her over his shoulder. A solid whack landed on her bottom as a giggle escaped her mouth. Joe's masculine laughter mixed with hers as he tossed her onto his bed. His hands peeled his shirt off as Amber leaned back on her elbows. "But I've made up my mind, honey. Fate dropped you in my path and I'm not going to look at the details. You make this place a home, Amber, so I'm asking you to stick around and help me fill up some of those bedrooms."

He wasn't asking her. Joe's voice was full of arrogant demand and the tone reminded her of a drill sergeant. Amber grinned as she considered the heated debates their life together was bound to be filled with. She lifted a finger at him.

"I'll make a demanding wife, Joe Lott."

"Dear God! I hope so!" His eyes lit with challenge.

He landed on the bed and cupped a breast with a firm hand. Amber sighed as his lips nibbled at hers before pushing them apart for his kiss.

Love wasn't just silly, it was corny and unexpected but most importantly, it was spontaneous. Her fingers threaded through his hair as she realized that this love was just perfect. Wedged right in between life's ups and downs there was Joe.

"I will never take it off."

"I love you, Little Red."

"Auburn!"

His fingers dipped down across her belly and found the soft curls at the top of her mound. His lips leaned towards her ear… "Red, my sassy Little Red." Joe leaned out the window. "Hey, Frank, tell your mama to marry me."

The tortoise snorted and pushed the basketball into his house. It was freshly painted with heat lamps attached to the top of it. Snip had painted a face on the basketball too. Frank ambled in behind his basketball as Joe wiggled his eyebrow at Amber. "I love Frank. I think we have a lot in common."

Well, they just might at that, but Amber giggled as she lay back across the satin bed covering. Dark eyes followed her every move as she smiled. Joe might favor her pet in a few ideas but he certainly chased his chosen partner a whole lot faster!

Enjoy this excerpt from

Beyond Boundaries
Breaking Boundaries

His hand came out and gently stroked the side of her face. Chenoa felt her eyes close as the pure pleasure of the touch captured her entire attention. His skin was hot too. His touch seemed to soothe her overheated face. The way his hand smelled was distantly aggressive. Every part of his body radiated his presence to her. Her eyes snapped open as her brain registered the amount of strength his scent seemed to declare.

Chenoa stepped back and shifted as her balance wavered. "You should not touch me." Her voice lacked any conviction. It was a mere whisper because Chenoa liked his touch. The promise he seemed to be declaring was attractive. It awakened a yearning deep inside her belly that twisted tighter with each new sensation.

"Why not, Chenoa?"

"Such touches are not meant to be displayed."

She was too hot with his eyes on her. The heat became worse as it spread to her body and down into her abdomen. A tiny pulse began throbbing in her center.

His huge hand wrapped around her wrist. The grip was solid yet only firm. He turned on a heel and took her with him. Chenoa found her feet hurrying to keep pace with his long legs.

Lee let her go the second the door closed behind him. He walked the few steps to his table to leave his helmet there. He turned to consider the object of his mental dilemma. His skin itched to get out of his uniform. Being in the mood for sex was one thing. This was need and it certainly went deeper than just the intercourse that would relieve his erection. He wanted to touch her, every last bit of her skin. Inhale its fragrance as he tasted her.

"Come over here and touch me."

Lee waited to see what she would do. She seemed poised on the edge of fleeing and he wanted to find the means of enticing her closer to him. Capturing her would be simple, but tempting her was so much more intense.

Chenoa looked at his huge frame. If she stepped closer he would be even larger, more powerful. The throbbing increased and sank lower inside her body, till the folds of her sex seemed too crowded and she shifted her thighs apart to relieve the pressure.

"Try it." Lee extended his hand, palm up to see what she'd do. Her eyes flicked over it and she lifted a slim hand toward him. Victory was swift but she didn't put her hand into his as Lee expected her to. Instead her sensitive fingertips traced over his palm and wrist in a teasing movement that was almost too delicate to feel.

Her fingertips were once again alive with sensation. Chenoa smiled at the pure pleasure she seemed to feel when their bare skin met. Her breasts rose beneath her dress as the nipples drew into tight little buttons.

Lee couldn't remember the last time he'd enjoyed such an innocent touch. He groaned as she ran her hand smoothly over his chest. The strong scent of her body filled his lungs making his body surge forward with the need to take. But having her approach him twisted his senses in an explosion of approval.

Lifting his hand, Lee gently tapped his lips. Her eyes darkened as the tip of her tongue appeared to run over her bottom lip.

"Kiss me, Chenoa."

She wanted to do just that. Wisdom tried to intrude but Chenoa brushed it aside. It simply felt correct to be in contact with him. His body was tense as he held iron control over his flesh. She found herself trusting in this man's ability to temper his strength.

She flattened both hands over his chest before rising onto her toes to comply. Lee clenched his hands into fists as he waited an eternity for that kiss. Her lips were soft as she tried to fit them to his. The contact broke as her toes refused to hold her up. Lee caught her bottom and raised her from the floor. He caught her gasps as his mouth took hers and boldly tasted the sweetness within.

Chenoa twisted as her body seemed to burn from within. She needed to be much closer to him. She sent her tongue searching for his as he turned and she felt the hard surface of the table beneath her bottom. He pressed toward her till her thighs parted to allow his hips to settle against her body. The layers of clothing seemed flimsy as the hard bulge of his sex pressed into her most tender flesh.

Yet it filled the ache throbbing there. Chenoa felt her hips thrust forward as pleasure shot deeply into her passage from the pressure. His firm hands slipped up her back before one gently cupped her breast. His thumb rubbed over her nipple making her gasp as pleasure erupted from the little point.

"Commander, sir?"

Lee growled. It was a menacing sound that frightened her with its level of ferocity. He abruptly turned to shield her with his back. The recruit standing in his doorway visibly paled.

"Excuse me, sir…Ah…Command is on the line."

Lee gave a hard nod and the man literally fled. He clenched his hands into fists as the scent of Chenoa's aroused body surrounded him. He couldn't think beyond the need to impale her. It went beyond intoxication. His sex raged with the knowledge that her body was wet and spread for him.

The words that came out of his mouth were vicious.

About the author:

I write to reassure myself that reality really is survivable. Between traffic jams and children's sporting schedules, there is romance lurking for anyone with the imagination to find it.

I spend my days making corsets and petticoats as a historical costumer. If you send me an invitation marked formal dress, you'd better give a date or I just might show up wearing my bustle.

I love to read a good romance and with the completion of my first novel, I've discovered I am addicted to writing these stories as well.

Dream big or you might never get beyond your front yard.

I love to hear what you think of my writing: Talk2MaryWine@hotmail.com.

Mary welcomes mail from readers. You can write to her c/o Ellora's Cave Publishing at 1056 Home Avenue, Akron OH 44310-3502.

Why an electronic book?

We live in the Information Age—an exciting time in the history of human civilization in which technology rules supreme and continues to progress in leaps and bounds every minute of every hour of every day. For a multitude of reasons, more and more avid literary fans are opting to purchase e-books instead of paperbacks. The question to those not yet initiated to the world of electronic reading is simply: *why?*

1. *Price.* An electronic title at Ellora's Cave Publishing and Cerridwen Press runs anywhere from 40-75% less than the cover price of the <u>exact same title</u> in paperback format. Why? Cold mathematics. It is less expensive to publish an e-book than it is to publish a paperback, so the savings are passed along to the consumer.

2. *Space.* Running out of room to house your paperback books? That is one worry you will never have with electronic novels. For a low one-time cost, you can purchase a handheld computer designed specifically for e-reading purposes. Many e-readers are larger than the average handheld, giving you plenty of screen room. Better yet, hundreds of titles can be stored within your new library—a single microchip. (Please note that Ellora's Cave and Cerridwen Press does not endorse any specific brands. You can check our website at www.ellorascave.com or

www.cerridwenpress.com for customer recommendations we make available to new consumers.)

3. *Mobility.* Because your new library now consists of only a microchip, your entire cache of books can be taken with you wherever you go.

4. *Personal preferences are accounted for.* Are the words you are currently reading too small? Too large? Too...**ANNOYING**? Paperback books cannot be modified according to personal preferences, but e-books can.

5. *Instant gratification.* Is it the middle of the night and all the bookstores are closed? Are you tired of waiting days—sometimes weeks—for online and offline bookstores to ship the novels you bought? Ellora's Cave Publishing sells instantaneous downloads 24 hours a day, 7 days a week, 365 days a year. Our e-book delivery system is 100% automated, meaning your order is filled as soon as you pay for it.

Those are a few of the top reasons why electronic novels are displacing paperbacks for many an avid reader. As always, Ellora's Cave and Cerridwen Press welcomes your questions and comments. We invite you to email us at service@ellorascave.com, service@cerridwenpress.com or write to us directly at: 1056 Home Ave. Akron OH 44310-3502.

erridwen, the Celtic Goddess of wisdom, was the muse who brought inspiration to storytellers and those in the creative arts. Cerridwen Press encompasses the best and most innovative stories in all genres of today's fiction. Visit our site and discover the newest titles by talented authors who still get inspired - much like the ancient storytellers did, once upon a time.